Praise for
Everything Here Is the Best Thing Ever
by Justin Taylor

"This spare, sharp book—Taylor's debut collection—document a deep authority on the unavoidable confusion of being young, disaffected, and human. . . . The most affecting stories in *Everything Here Is the Best Thing Ever* are as unpredictable as a careening drunk. They leave us with the heavy residue of an unsettling strangeness, and a new voice that readers—and writers, too—might be seeking out for decades to come."
—*New York Times Book Review*

"Justin Taylor is a master of the modern snapshot."
—*Los Angeles Times*

"Taylor's superb debut short story collection is explorative and fresh with well-crafted empathic characters. . . . Each story is spare and clean and speaks the truth in beautiful resonant prose."
—*Publishers Weekly*

"In his first book of short stories, Taylor hones a dark-humored and character-themed collection in the tradition of Mary Gaitskill's *Bad Behavior* or Denis Johnson's *Jesus' Son*."
—*Oxford American*

"These short fictions by Justin Taylor give such a convincing account of the rough crossing of young adulthood that they practically induce seasickness. For his youthful protagonists, identity—emotional, intellectual, sexual—is unstable, constantly in motion."
—*Boston Globe*

"Beautiful lines leap from the pages, and we gladly enter Taylor's vivid world, even as it transforms what we know about ourselves and others into something slippery and ever-changing."
—*Penthouse*

"Taylor's characters would like for time to both speed up and slow down—an impossible, inevitable wish that makes the moments he captures worth savoring."

—*BookForum*

"These stories of Gen Y, told with panache, dark humor, and technical flash will delight short fiction fans of all ages."

—*Booklist*

"Whether Taylor is exploring youth, human bonds, or fantastical scenarios, he displays a gift for illuminating the connections between the mundane and the grotesque."

—*Time Out* (New York)

"Taylor flirts with poetic language, teasing us with lines so lusciously packed that even a tattoo's description can set the page on fire."

—*Bookslut*

"Justin Taylor does irony and snark and thwarted idealism uncommonly well. . . . My pen underlined often."

—*The Huffington Post*

"Dazzling. . . . Taylor deftly captures the peculiar rhythms of the American vernacular."

—*SEE Magazine*

"The book I keep comparing his collection to is another debut, Philip Roth's *Goodbye, Columbus* . . . a fantastic debut collection."

—*PANK Magazine*

"A book filled with stories so clean and focused that they could have been the product of decades of work."

—*Creative Loafing*

"After reading the whole collection I have to tell you, there's no fiction writer I know with more promise, and more daring, than Justin Taylor right at this minute."

—Kevin Killian

Bill Hayward

About the Author

JUSTIN TAYLOR's fiction and nonfiction have been widely published in journals, magazines, and Web sites, including *The Believer*, *The Nation*, *The New York Tyrant*, the *Brooklyn Rail*, *The Oxford American*, and National Public Radio. A coeditor of *The Agriculture Reader* and a contributor to HTMLGIANT, Taylor lives in Brooklyn. He is the author of *Everything Here Is the Best Thing Ever*, a *New York Times Book Review* Editors' Choice. This is his first novel.

THE
GOSPEL
OF
ANARCHY

Also by Justin Taylor

FICTION

Everything Here Is the Best Thing Ever

POETRY

More Perfect Depictions of Noise

AS EDITOR

Come Back, Donald Barthelme

The Apocalypse Reader

The Word Made Flesh (with Eva Talmadge)

THE
GOSPEL
OF
ANARCHY

a novel

JUSTIN TAYLOR

HARPER  PERENNIAL

NEW YORK • LONDON • TORONTO • SYDNEY • NEW DELHI • AUCKLAND

HARPER ⬤ PERENNIAL

HarperCollins books may be purchased for educational, business, or sales promotional use. For information please write: Special Markets Department, HarperCollins Publishers, 10 East 53rd Street, New York, NY 10022.

FIRST EDITION

Designed by Justin Dodd

Library of Congress Cataloging-in-Publication Data is available upon request.

ISBN 978-0-06-188182-4

11 12 13 14 15   OV/RRD   10 9 8 7 6 5 4 3 2 1

For Abraham

For what else should we pursue, if not happiness? If something isn't valuable because we find meaning and joy in it, then what could possibly make it important? How could abstractions like "responsibility," "order," or "propriety" possibly be more important than the real needs of the people who invented them? Should we serve employers, parents, the State, God, capitalism, moral law, causes, movements, "society" before *ourselves? Who taught you that, anyway?*

The CrimethInc. Collective, *Days of War, Nights of Love*

Christianity is the only religion on earth that has felt that omnipotence made God incomplete. Christianity alone has felt that God, to be wholly God, must have been a rebel as well as a king.

—G. K. Chesterton, *Orthodoxy*

SUMMER, 1999

THE CONFESSIONS

I worked at the survey center in the Seagle Building, which stands eleven full stories on the north side of University Avenue, halfway between the eastern edge of campus and downtown. Excepting the Beaty Towers, a pair of Soviet bloc–style dorms built in the late '60s, it was—and still is—the tallest building in all of Gainesville. Our offices were on the ground floor. We contracted with government programs and private insurers. We wore headsets, hooked into desktop computers; we felt the heat of the machines through our pant legs, even as their cooling fans keened louder, quickening their endless spin. We stared into boxy monitors with dull green screens, sat tucked behind half-height cubicle walls of coarse gray fabric flecked with colored bits like tiny festive mistakes.

The machines autodialed while we thumbed magazines. Junk stuff, mostly—*Vogue*, *Spin*, *Esquire*, maybe a *News-*

week now and then, or *Time*. The magazines, page-worn and out of date, were supplied by the office, piled on a counter in the break room. Management didn't want us reading books, or anything assigned. So no Norton Anthology, no sheaf of double-sided runoffs held together with a worry-bent staple. If you had a highlighter out, you were busted. (A dropout, none of this was a problem for me.) We had to be alert, poised, ready to get on the line and start talking to whoever answered the phone we'd dialed, or else cut the call off if a machine clicked on. We could not, therefore, afford the distraction of anything with depth.

It was a roomful of students and ex-students, managed by listless postgrads with timorous seniority. Our job was to wait for a live human voice and when we got one, to read to it the information on the screen. We were selling nothing, asking only for time and honesty.

We spoke to retirees, recovering addicts, people on the welfare rolls, on parole; recent hospital releases eager to rate their inpatient experience—seven, no, no, six, I guess, okay, is there a six and a half? I'm sorry, ma'am, but there is no six and a half. They asked us questions we could not answer, say, about the status of their claim, or what this information will be used for. Statistical purposes. We reassured them. We assuaged. Your anonymity is safe. We add your numbers to the great database.

We used a modulated tone, a cool-to-the-touch tone. The voice of condolences offered on behalf of an absent friend. We only had jobs because it was understood that these people would not take calls from robots. You hear an automated voice and assume someone is trying to get you into a timeshare, raise money for a congressman, sell tickets for a cruise. And also because someone had to log all the answers. The people, it was felt, could not be trusted to correctly punch in the numbers corresponding to their choices on their touchtone phones.

I didn't read while I worked, not even the magazines. I just sat and watched—the screen, or the other callers. I peeked around my gray walls. I gazed and surveyed. Here was a girl with a Pantene-sleek ponytail that started high on her head and went halfway down her back; sorority Greek on a thin gold chain, the characters perfectly centered in the scoop neck of a pale pink shirt. A gangly freshman guy, acne-scarred, five eleven, perpetually anemic-seeming in black jeans like burnt sticks. The fat girl with Coke-bottle glasses and a torn blue windbreaker; she never brought anything to read, either. She just sat there, silent and still, Zening out on her green screen. I wondered what she did when she got a call through—if she could rouse herself from those green depths and actually speak—but I never sat close enough to listen. A whole roomful of us. Rooms, actually. There were three full rooms. You got a different station every time. Some people, I imagine, made friends.

If you don't unmute the headset right when you hear the phone pick up, then the person you've called hears the little click of you clicking the unmute button and then that person thinks you are a robot whose recording has just clicked on.

They played the same game with us that we played with their answering machines: if it sounds automatic, dump it.

The people we were calling didn't have vacation days piling up. They did not wish to be selected for a special offer, four nights five days, continental breakfast, Disney World, whatever it was. They were looking for overtime, not time off. We had to let them know right away that quote *this is not a sales call.* We were people just like them, going about our business, collecting only that which we needed, and which was free to give, which is not to say it was often given freely.

People resented us, and rightly. We were wound-pokers, interlopers in their shattered lives, and the untone in which we probed was a compounding offense. We asked them about the last time they'd had steady work. How long since the coverage ran out? Your anonymity, we said, again, is assured, though if they'd thought about it they'd have realized that implicit in the set of questions and the fact of our calling was how much we already had on them. They were angry; they were outraged. They yelled at us, called us things.

We were forbidden to be provoked by them, or say anything at all not printed on our screens. Don't get baited. Don't engage. And some hung up, but these were relatively few. Surprisingly few, or maybe not so surprisingly. We spoke, after all, with a vague but convincing air of authority, and people suspected that we had no actual power over them (we didn't), but they weren't prepared to test that theory and be wrong. These were people who were behind on payments, who patronized check-cashing stores. Some were gracious,

decent to us, even kind, maybe pleased to have been asked
to share or just to have someone to talk to. These were also
few. Everyone else said we were interrupting dinner. They
said we had no business, no right. They sputtered and swore.
And then they told us everything we asked.

At home there was no conversation. No back and forth. No
feigned ease, no modulated voice. No voice, period. Silence
reigned. Quiet clicks. The world opened up to me through a
small bright window, my personal laptop computer, which
was of course too heavy and ran too hot to actually keep
on my lap, not that I wanted it there. I had to use a plug-in
trackball mouse because I couldn't get the hang of the touch-
pad thing. The laptop was barely a year old, still more or
less state-of-the-art, and had pride of place on the desk in
my living room, where I sat and surfed a wave that never
crested, climbed a mountain that never peaked. Curved,
oiled, chesty, slick, spread; sometimes I imagined the girls
in a kind of march, an endless parade celebrating—what?
Themselves, I guess, or me.

They bit their lower lips and looked away from the camera. Soft-focus, standing half behind a gauzy white curtain
through which a clump of pubic hair is basically an idea about
itself. Or harsh light on razor rash. Or a sequence in which
three short-haired, flat-chested Russians swim in a shallow
pond, then towel each other off in tall weedy grass. Thick
rugs on hardwood floors. Women relaxing and relaxed. Natural breasts, floppy and pale on a tanned body: she stands

next to a palm tree, one hand on the trunk, she's leaning—
this is the relaxed part, a woman is taking it *easy*—the other
hand on her hip, thumb inside the waist of her bikini bottom,
like who knows what she might do next? But I know what she
might do next. What else is there to do next?

A girl wearing reading glasses, a backward baseball cap,
and nothing else. Her eyes are squinched shut, mouth wide
open and stuffed full, nose half disappeared into some guy's
auburn bush, in what appears to be one or the other of their
dorms—UMass Amherst, if the pennant on the wall is to be
believed.

Rooms washed in evening, in morning light. In full ugly
Texas sun. Asians in stilettos. Blacks in nurse uniforms.

Every image was a whole world, complete, unfolding. But
the sites were always trying to tell me what I was seeing,
frame my experience with narrative, override or manage it
somehow. They—the sites—were heavy on text; lousy with
it, in fact, and choked with ads. It was worse than cable. Hell,
it was worse than talk radio. I hated all of it: the captions,
backstories, scene-setting, conceits and premises, banners
that flashed. And the cartoonish language, the gleeful gild-
ing of the filth. The sites spoke only of miracles. They told
me that what I saw was even hotter, dirtier, stranger, than I
already thought it was. And they told me I hadn't seen the
half of it. They told me I was about to get my mind blown—
better, faster, again—around the next digital bend. There
was more, always more and better, just waiting. It was one
big medicine show.

The hackers had homemade programs, which they called proggies, and each proggie had some stupid scary-sounding name that paid homage to the miasma of gangsta rap and Mountain Dew from which it had been born. HaVok, AO-Hell, Fate X. The proggies enabled the hackers—or any kid who got hold of the software—to log on via fake and therefore untraceable screen names. They wielded godlike powers; for example, they could boot users out of chat rooms and usurp the freed-up space themselves. The hackers would go from room to room, recording all the names of all the users in each room. When they felt that they had enough names, they'd send out a mass email with a picture attached. The idea was that if everybody on the list replied with one picture, then everybody on the list would get however many free pictures. Of course not everybody responded, and some people only offered their "commons" to the share lists (sometimes the hackers tracked these people down and punished them for being skinflints), but there would be hundreds of names on each list. The Amway logic of the thing actually worked, and the result was cornucopia. It was the prosperity gospel. My apartment building had just installed broadband, complex-wide. I had never seen anything like this speed. It was a state of perpetual overload, and there was no reason—no way, in a sense—to ever stop. A single list might linger on for days.

With my name affixed to a list—or several—and the first fruits of the harvest starting to tick in, I would minimize (though never exit) the chat room window, maximize the mailbox window in its place, and begin.

Some of the sites were in Spanish, or Russian, and that was better, because I didn't know those languages. The text became less like an interruption then, more like background noise, patterned wallpaper. The text tried to reach you but couldn't, and so you remained free.

Eventually I made my way to message boards, AOL chat rooms. These were of two kinds. Public rooms were established, maintained, and moderated by the company. "Automotive." "Singles." "Baltimore." Private rooms were unlisted, and anyone could make them. They weren't password protected, but in order to get to one, you had to know its name. All the rooms—public and private—capped at twenty-two users at a time. If a public room had no users, it just sat there, but a private room would disappear. Of course the very next time somebody typed that name in, the room would reinvent itself, and there that guy would be in it, all alone.

Think of a likely-sounding name—"nakedgirls," let's say, or "amateurs," or simply "pics." Then throw a number behind it—"jpeg14"—because dozens of these rooms ran at once, and the low numbers almost always had the virtual equivalent of lines around the block. Most people used the chat room to shout out what they had or what they wanted: "cheerleaders," "double-team," "teens." Then the like-minded would work their trades out in private, over IM.

I didn't do any of that. It was more noise, the opposite of what I required. What I did was fight my way into a room, any room was fine, and then I sat there in silence, waiting for the hackers.

A girl with a perfect, pale ass like an upside-down heart is standing in the doorway of a bedroom. Her own, it seems fair to assume. Her hair is tied back, appears wet. The picture is cockeyed, suggesting that the photographer was a little off balance, maybe snagged the shot while in motion, snuck it on the fly. We can see into the girl's room, somewhat, around her shape and through her legs. There's a loud pink bedspread, mussed. All kinds of stuff on the floor.

Every single one of these images was a betrayal. Privacies violated, trusts broken. That was the real frame narrative, the superstructure, and this knowledge made them so much more powerful. They stank of aura.

Except that wasn't always the case, was it? A woman sitting in a rolling chair in a home office, a converted den, wearing a tank top only, tipping the chair back, legs spread wide, playing with herself with one hand and holding up a sign with the other: the name of some Usenet group, the date of the picture, the words *#1 Fan.* Swingers. Exhibitionists. *Baby, you know how many people are gonna see this and get themselves off to it?* No, baby, tell me, tell me all about it. Okay, baby. Now tell me again.

So there were two narratives, actually, of equal but inverse and irreconcilable power. It was either *She never wanted this,* or else it was *She got exactly what she wanted.* You had to decide for yourself. You had to make it up as you went along.

Topless girls in front of sinks, their own or that of some hotel room, blowing their hair out, brushing teeth, looking away from the camera or sidelong into it with an expression like *Seriously, Anthony, would you knock it off?*

In bed, fully nude, reclining, dark hair in a bun and a deep natural tan, legs crossed at the ankles, blanket scrunched down by her feet, weirdly demure, a single dollop of jism near her pierced navel like a pale moon orbiting a silver-ringed planet, one hand behind her head. In the other hand, a bulky gray cellular phone, which indicated that the image was from at least four or five years ago. And where was this girl now? Still with the guy who'd snapped the photo, or had their breakup been the trigger for his sharing?

I copied and saved my favorites so I could look at them again later. One folder, holding all I'd culled from the sites and from the lists. A window on my own desktop. No interference. No connection at all required. I could unplug the broadband, if I wanted, and just cycle through the thousand favorites I already had. But of course I didn't do that. I minimized the whole AOL window, but inside it, tucked away, the mailbox was open and the chat was still logged on. I changed my desktop background to pure white. I hid all the other icons, and the toolbar, too. I opened the image browser. I pressed the little box that maximizes.

Here they were, surrounded with plain white pixels, pure radiance, mystic roses at the center of my heaven, burning bushes (I mean no pun). I stared until I saw clear through them and into their constitutive brightness. I aimed back at my own chest, and cleaned up with tissues that saturated and wept apart. As my frequency increased, so did my stamina, and my issuance came in watery, thin ropes. There were paper fibers spun up in the hair on my stomach.

I discovered the slide show option in a pull-down menu in the image browser. Click. It was synesthetic, full frontal sex light the color of the feeling of office air, white recirculation, bodies made of light, ever present for endless consumption yet never themselves consumed—skin that looked sweat-slick but was in fact cool to the touch, or would have been if it had been in fact touchable, made of something other than computer glass and unconsummated light. Skin smooth as keyboard keys, dry and noiseless as the planetlike spinning of the trackball in its cradle.

What had been born of boredom and curiosity, then mutated into enthusiasm and honest perversion, then refined itself further into a kind of connoisseurship, now seemed to have transcended all these things and become something else, which delivered neither pleasure nor its opposite. Its only truly novel aspect, at this point, was the sheer monstrosity of its breadth—the perpetual beckon of more and more. Even to call it compulsion would be to make it seem more dire, and thus significant, than it actually was. I had a habit. That was all.

Rock star head shots plucked from the pages of glossy magazines. They taped these to their walls. Or rappers. Inspirational posters in cheap frames. A lot of people don't shut their TV off. They get caught up in the excitement and, forgotten, ignored, on it blares. Or maybe it's muted. How could the image tell you? Or maybe they've got the volume turned way up so whoever is in the next room can't hear. These are just for me, he told her, just for *us*. She gave him that look. He thought she wasn't going to, but then she tugged at her blouse hem, tentative, testing, a toe dipped in water, and he knew she would. She did. Girls who squinch their eyes shut. Girls who stare back up at you, staring you down. "You." Shaved or unshorn, or better still—shaving. Caught in the act. Process and method. So drunk she can't stand. Here's the two of us in Cabo. Okay, now here's one of just her. Took this while she was sleeping. Shoulda thought twice, you cheating bitch. You slut. I love it when you call me that. Girls in showers, one arm across the breasts and the other waving away the camera, but smiling—exasperated, tolerant. *Are you fucking kidding me, Anthony?* Baby, it's cool, just be cool.

Stuffed animals, stray socks and shoes, and books— math textbooks, *Moby-Dick*, Harry Potter, Stephen King, *The Complete Idiot's Guide to* fill in the blank. Bibles. Bedside clutter on low tables. Human detritus—mundane and fascinating. The way things accreted and gathered. Loose change, heaped or stacked neatly. Watches, matches, rings.

The insider knowledge, routine his-and-hers smells. Everything you've seen so many times it's basically invisible, or else it's the one thing that you *always* notice but never mention. The way he holds me. Her neck mole. The humdrum fuck. A little bored, a little mad at each other, but it's Friday night and . . . The calendar with tomorrow's date circled— your doctor's appointment, our concert tickets. A guitar on a stand against the far wall by the window. You never play anymore. Find me the time and I'll play. A computer monitor, ancient, size of a microwave, eating up all available space on a beat-up black Formica corner desk. Discarded clothes, torn frenzied from the body—or is that laundry left undone? A framed photograph on the nightstand: child with beagle. I'm tired. But do you still want to? I mean, you *do* want to, right? Because we don't have to. I want to do what you want to do. Digital alarm clocks. Record collections. Warn me before you come.

This was my life. Length and breadth, scope and weft. Reflex action. An object in motion. I had let January's official end of an already-dead-in-the-water relationship become an excuse for letting my grades go to hell, which resulted in my dropping the entire spring semester. Now it was the dead of summer. I had to re-enroll, sign up for classes, do the whole back-on-track bit. Problem was, the mere thought of stepping back onto campus, much less into the office of some admissions counselor, with her cat poster and candy dish, induced apoplexy. There would be forms to fill out. I would have to choose classes—be more interested in one thing than some other. I'd have to be interested, period. I couldn't visualize that. All that I could generate, in fact, was TV static, accompanied by the rough white noise of the sea, as if a pair of conch shells were strapped to my head. It was enough to send me right back to my computer, for another protracted round of chafing succor. I was twenty-one years old.

I had a one-bedroom apartment, five-eighths of a degree in the liberal arts and exactly one core conviction, which was that I would not move back to South Florida, where an unchanged childhood bedroom waited like an armed bear trap. And so I went to work.

I was on the phone with an old woman. She had started out eager to tell me about her buying habits, but now she was getting flustered. This was my fault, in a sense. The royal me. It was the annual state consumer statistics survey and we had gotten onto a long sequence about driving habits and preferences in gasoline. Did she know the difference between super and regular? Did she care? About how much driving did she do in a given week? Month? There were literally dozens of questions in this line. It was a long survey that few people agreed to take.

What kind of person, cold-called at six-fifteen in the evening on a Wednesday, agrees to sit for a forty-five-minute interrogation? We had established her widowhood earlier. I'd even bent the rules and indulged her in brief agreement on Earl's having been a good man. Some three years gone now, she told me. She was in a small town in the west-central part of the state. She was horse country people: honest and openhearted and a little dumb, spending her golden years not in repose on some porch as she and Earl had dreamed, but instead in a modest trailer—that is, modest by the already modest standards of trailer homes. Fixed income in a truckstop town, her eyesight failing. People and things were blobs to her, shapes without edges in a landscape of colorful mud.

She had her neighbors, of course, and some people from the church. The kids come to visit when they can.

There was a flaw in the programming of the survey. That much was clear. They were designed like choose-your-own-adventure stories, and the system should have offered me an option to tell it that she did not drive, period. Frequently, somewhat frequently, occasionally, or seldom. Those were my choices, or rather, hers—(A) through (D). Do you want me to repeat the choices I have listed?

"I keep saying," she said. There was a quaver in her voice. "I don't drive no more. I *can't.*" She was going to start crying. How many times would I make her tell me she was going blind?

"I'm sorry," I said. "Look, let's just skip these." I gave her (D)s for everything. Isn't never a kind of seldom?

When the survey finally wrapped up, nearly twenty minutes later, she wished me all the best of luck with my studies, because, she said, she could hear in my voice that I was a smart young man who worked hard. It was my turn to choke a little, but I thanked her for having hung in with me to the end and wished her all the very best. She told me to call her back with new surveys anytime, and even though the odds of her getting called by our company again were decent, the odds of me being selected by the system to be the caller were next to zero. And even if such a thing were possible it was almost certainly against some protocol or other. I told her I would make a note and be sure to. We thanked each other again and then I let her go.

I took my headset off and paused the machine's dialing mechanism, because I could feel that I was being watched. I turned around to face Steven, the shift manager. He was five nine, heavyset, broken out, and about my age, but somehow very grown-up looking. He wore ugly sweaters in all weather, to hide his man-boobs. Today's was maroon.

"Come on into the office, David," he said.

He spoke in an angry hush. His breath smelled, but not like anything. It just smelled. I followed him out of the calling room, a quick walk of shame.

"You know what you did," he said. "I assume you know."

"I know what I did," I said.

"Nobody here is out to get you," he said. "We monitor our callers at random. This is nothing you don't already know."

"To ensure quality, I get that. You have to do your job."

"And you have to do *your* job, David. Yes?"

"Yes, but—"

"You stopped reading the questions. You filled in answers. You tampered with results."

"If you were listening to that part of the conversation then you heard that woman's voice. Did you hear her voice?"

"David, people hire this company because they expect a certain level—"

"Hey," I said. "I wasn't going to make an old woman cry. You can't make me do that. Your survey's all fucked."

"Don't raise your voice, David," Steven said.

"Look," I said.

"No," he said. "You look. The surveys come to us from tech. Copy produces the questions; tech does the coding and builds the survey. You conduct the survey. Processing processes the results. That's what this job is. It might not be glamorous but that's what it is."

"An old woman," I said. "Crying."

"I'm sending you home for the day," Steven said. "Go grab your stuff and then clock out."

"I broke a rule, I get it, okay. You want to send me home, okay. But at least tell me you heard that woman on the phone. You heard what I heard."

"I asked you to leave, David. And now I'm telling you."

He wouldn't say it. I went back into the calling room to get my backpack, which didn't have anything in it except the keys to my bike lock and the keys to my house. When I'd begun here I'd always brought plenty to read. When had that stopped, exactly? And why was I still bringing the empty bag? It didn't matter, but then, not much did. I slung the weightless, shapeless thing over one shoulder. I left.

I had some pictures of my own. Three, exactly—Polaroids of Becky. We started dating sophomore year, lasted through early junior spring. Ancient history now. She'd sent them to me the previous summer, when we were apart from each other. Not that we suffered and yearned so much. She went back to her parents' place in Tallahassee, and I stayed in Gainesville. Three hours' drive, more or less, from here to there. We spent most of our weekends together, in one town or the other, and though we obviously both preferred my very parentless apartment, I can honestly say that I didn't dislike spending time with her folks, a pair of liberal do-gooder doctors who had met in the Peace Corps and were almost as still-with-it as they thought they were.

Our only real separation occurred in the month of August, when Becky and her whole family left for three weeks in Europe to celebrate the happy combination of her parents' thirtieth anniversary and her older brother's entering medical school that fall. The weekend before her departure she had planned to come down to Gainesville. But then on that Thursday she'd accidentally backed into a light pole while parking her car at a movie theater. The damage was only cosmetic, she was sure, but her father wasn't going to let her take the thing out on a highway until he'd had it looked at, and since they were leaving in just a few days it would not be looked at until after they got back. Neither would he let her have one of the other cars to make the trip with.

I offered to come to her, but that wasn't good, either. Her brother was home, and everyone was in a tizzy with packing, and it was just too much trouble, her parents felt. We settled for long daily talks on the phone, until she left the following Tuesday. Two days after that an envelope addressed from her to me arrived in the mail. Inside of it were the three Polaroids, with one word written in black marker on the back of each one. I'LL. MISS. YOU.

When we broke up, better than half a year later—now nearly half a year ago—she did not ask me for them back.

Probably, they had slipped her mind entirely, as they had for a long time mine.

The first was a head shot: smiling, bare shoulders shiny, hair wet. The second picture was a right-facing profile of her torso. She had small breasts almost overwhelmed by her large dark areolae, but her nipples themselves were small, too, and flattish. They hardly stood up, even when she was at her most aroused. She had arched her back. I wondered—not for the first time—how many pictures she had taken before settling on these three. What had gone through her mind as she'd done it? And why this? I had never asked her to pose for me. It was all her own idea. She had one of those small sexy bellies that skinny girls have, the ones they're always talking about trying to get rid of and you never know what you're supposed to say back. It wasn't even a belly, really; it was more like a slight grade— the organic slope of her torso out toward her belly button, that little jewel of space, that niche, and then back in toward her sex, which was not depicted. She was wearing a pair of my boxer shorts, the waist of which had been folded down several times so that they rode low beneath her prominent hip bones, and the very top edge of her pubic hair peeked out from the fabric. The third picture was a close-up. Her vulva held agape by the first and third fingers of her left hand—the nails had been recently manicured, but not painted any color, only glazed—and the middle finger dipped inside herself up to the second joint.

I held the photographs in my hands and flipped through them. I spread them out on the computer desk in front of the keyboard. I plugged in my scanner.

I was suddenly tired—exhausted, *sick*—of playing the vulture, the hyena of intimacy. Well, I had had a life too, once, and here was the evidence. Let some other lonely asshole debase himself over *my* artifacts, *my* souvenirs.

I scanned all three photographs, opened the first one as a bitmap file in Paintbrush, drew a rectangle over Becky's eyes, then filled that space in with solid black. I saved the file, converted it back to a JPEG, and then sent all three pictures out to the next list I found myself on. A little traveling pack.

Two days later, on a different list, she came back to me. Someone had passed her along, billed as his own current girlfriend. What was interesting, though, was that the guy had sent only that first one, the one with no actual nudity. The bare shoulders, I guessed. The shiny skin. The black-out rectangle. Yes, I could see it now, how that was the most alluring, how it hinted at things no triple-X full-reveal ever could.

Or maybe he was just a wheeler-dealer looking to pique interest and make trades. Hey man, I've never seen *her* before. You got any more where that came from? Yeah, man, but what do *you* got?

I downloaded the picture. I had sent the images out as "exgf" 1, 2, and 3, so as far as cyberspace had known she was nameless. But her name was Ramona now, according to the file. I let the light that was her burn through me. I pretended she was someone I had never known and tried to scare up some plausible fuck fantasy about her, like I had gotten into the habit of doing with all the other girls. It wasn't cunt I was interested in, not anymore. It wasn't tits or the hot wet dark of her mouth. It wasn't any of the things the lists or the sites wanted me to think about her—these things I already knew for certain and yet struggled to remember and then, remembering, could no longer believe because of who was telling them to me. I knew now they all were liars. And not just *that* they were, but *how*. The thick line across her eyes was everything. To have spared her that much, even if only *just* that much. But in so doing I had made her anybody—nobody. She was raw material now. She was YOUR FACE HERE.

I stood up from my computer chair and kicked it away behind me. I throbbed, skull crown to toe tips, and bit through my lower lip and wanted to shut my eyes while I came but would not let myself so much as blink and stared into the black rectangle until it reversed itself. When I did look away, finally, the afterimage stayed at the center of my vision, a fiery brightness that dissipated slowly, like water down a half-clogged drain, and through that receding curtain I watched my slime slide down the bright screen and pool on the keyboard and seep in. I folded the laptop closed, unplugged it, and took it into the bathroom. I plugged the drain and turned the water on. I filled the tub to the brim. This took a few minutes and during this time I drummed my fingers on the lid of the machine. But I was not nervous. I had already done the irrevocable thing. This was just a showy finish, an improvised ritual of consecration. The machine thrummed in my hands, plastic hot to the touch where the battery and fan were. I dropped it in and stepped back from the splash. I shut the bathroom door behind me, hoping for a spark that would send the whole complex up, but knowing I didn't have that much luck coming. I got dressed and left the house.

But where to go?

All the main roads in Gainesville are named for the towns that they lead to. Archer, Waldo, Williston, Hawthorne, Newberry. Nobody ever meant for here to be anyplace special. It exists because someone wanted the county seat on the new railroad line, which Newmansville wasn't. So they founded this place, named for an Indian killer, General Edmund Gaines, and made it the new seat of Alachua County, itself named for the Indians that General Gaines slaughtered. That's as much as I know about Gainesville, other than that these days it's the closest thing to an urban center between Jacksonville and Orlando, if you don't count Tampa, which is off to the west. That's all because of UF, the University of Florida, which is one of the largest schools in the whole country. Fifty thousand students, give or take, nearly half the population of the city. The school is more than the main thing here. It's the only thing. If you don't go there or teach there, then you fix the cars of those who do, or you own a restaurant with a sign reading STUDENT DISCOUNT SHOW ID taped in its front window, or if you don't own it then your uncle does, and you hate working for the SOB but who else is going to hire you? The school is inescapable, like the humidity, like every shadow points back to the sun, and the locals hate the way the kids drink and fuck shit up on the weekends, and the kids look down on the townies, but the football stadium holds eighty thousand, and every game sells out.

I didn't want to walk around campus, so I went the other way. East on University Avenue, past fast-food joints, a liquor store, a gas station, an office supply, the fucking Seagle Building, dim bars with muddy guitar washing from their propped front doors. I walked through the modest downtown, a couple of nice restaurants and frat-favored dance clubs, that's about all it was, give or take a coffee shop and an art house movie theater. I walked past the library, out to where East University becomes Hawthorne Road, and the sidewalk grew cracked and weed-split, and the homes needed paint jobs they wouldn't get. I kept on Hawthorne to where it crossed Waldo Road, which bears northeast. I stood at this intersection, contemplating my choices—two places I didn't know anything about, both of which were positively nowhere, and neither of which I had any business being. Waldo had the regional airport. I could watch planes land and take off, crop dusters or whatever it was they had. Not that any would be out at this hour. (Not that I was on some schedule.) My only real plan was to walk all night.

I turned back, thinking maybe I'd end up at the school after all.

Maybe I would find an unlocked hall to shuffle around in. Or I could stand outside the admissions building, have myself a little revelation about doing the right thing in life. At the very least there would be the empty campus streets, and the wooded paths between the clusters of buildings. The paths were paved, and, since the Danny Rolling murders, now almost ten years ago, garishly lit. I thought I might end up at the bat house, over at the far end of campus, by the lake. The bats were protected or researched or something, I didn't really know, but I knew that watching the bats rouse at sunset and take to the sky was a popular evening activity—something everybody got around to doing, sooner or later, though so far I hadn't. But didn't it stand to reason that there would be a similar viewing at sunrise? I could walk around Lake Alice, then go to the bat house at daybreak and watch the dark thousands as they flooded back into their stilt-built wooden mansion, a black river in the bruised and brightening sky.

I turned off University Avenue to walk down something that wasn't sure if it was a street or an alley. The backyards of the houses that faced Southwest First were to my left side, and the back end of a strip mall that faced University was on my right. It was a rutted, potholed, gouged-out road—treacherous for bicycles, barely wide enough for two cars to pass each other. If you didn't want to park behind the strip mall, there was really no reason to be on this street, which as far as I knew didn't even have a name. I had the whole dismal scene to myself. Or thought I did, until I came within range of the smallish green dumpster behind the Gyro Plus, and noticed its being attended by a pair of urgent-looking punks. I understood their concern. The alley was well lit and if a cop happened to pass by they'd be nabbed for trespassing, vagrancy—who knew what else?

The one serving as lookout was a girl about my own age, though this in itself was nothing special in a college town. Everyone here is about our age, and anyone who's not—you just see through them. I was at the approximate peak of my visibility. In a year you'd be able to read a street sign through me; in three years I wouldn't register at all. In the meantime, however, here I was.

The girl seemed scrappy, wore black jeans and boots, and a green-and-black band tee shirt underneath a beat-to-hell leather jacket that was probably supposed to make her look tough, but it was outsize, hung loose on her thin frame, and made her actually look a little bit like she had been rooting through her big brother's closet, playing dress-up. Her pursed lips were nearly white, and her gaze was steely, cold; or she wanted me to think that it was. I could feel her sizing me up as I approached. I kept my own eyes cast down. I wanted her to know I was no threat. We were two ships. But I did look up for a second, couldn't help stealing a glance, and saw her lean over toward the dumpster and whisper to the man who, I could now see, was half in and half out of the thing, headfirst, his legs bicycling wildly in the air in what I understood was only a parody of struggle. He'd posted her as guard and now would not heed her warning. Giving her grief was obviously part of the pleasure he took in this mission. They were already behind me when I heard him shout, "Score! Dining room bag!"

I froze in my footsteps, then turned back.

"Thomas?" I called, my voice louder than I'd meant it to be. The girl looked positively frantic now. There was a nasty clang from within the dumpster. He'd hit his head clambering out. In one hand he held a big white sack of garbage with a hole torn in it; with the other he rubbed a spot on the back of his head. We were maybe fifteen feet apart, staring at each other.

"What the fuck?" the girl said. Thomas burst out laughing.

"Maybe the crazy bitch is right," he said to her. "This is *two* amazing scores in one night. Maybe there really *is* a God."

The girl's eyes went to slits, as if she were zeroing in on a target, and Thomas seemed to change in an instant as well. His joke had stung her, clearly, but somehow her flash of anger, instead of putting him on the defensive, had stoked his own. He glared back at her, and something ugly and silent passed between them, like a shape in fog. The silence spooled out. We were all just standing there. As quickly as I'd been discovered, I felt forgotten, and thought I might say good-bye and get back to walking. Or maybe saying hello in the first place had been my mistake, and it was better now to simply go without another word. But then the girl conceded the staring contest and turned away from Thomas to me. Her lips eased out of their grimace, an act that seemed to require substantial effort. But she did it, and took a few steps forward, and stuck a filthy hand out toward me, and said, "Hi, I'm Liz. You guys know each other?"

"We grew up together," Thomas said, before I could say anything. I nodded as I closed the distance between us. I took her hand in mine. She had a firm grip, and for a moment squeezed very tightly, as if daring me to challenge her strength. I didn't. We pumped, the grime on her hand squishing between our palms. "K through twelve," Thomas continued. "The whole bit." He was trying to put some distance between the three of us and whatever had just happened or nearly happened between the two of them.

"It's true," I said. "We're from the same neighborhood, down south near Miami. Our families even caravanned up here together on freshman drop-off day."

"Hah, yeah—I'd forgotten about that. The long shining line of station wagons. That was us."

"So why haven't we met him before?" Liz asked Thomas.

"We just—"

"Lost touch," I offered.

"Yeah, that's about right," Thomas said. "I dropped out, a disgrace to all good and diligent bourgeoisie everywhere, and moved in with you assholes"—he gestured at Liz—"but David stuck to the plan like he was supposed to. Didn't you? So you must be graduating this year. Gonna move back to Miami, flip the old law/medicine coin? Or did that decision already get made? You could have done some summer classes a few times, I guess, finished a year early. Why, you could be thinking about the bar right now, couldn't you?"

"Actually," I said, "I'm on a br— I dropped out."

"No shit," he said, seeming genuinely impressed. "For what? You go to India and find yourself or something?"

"I've just been hanging around. Working. Except I quit my job, so." I shrugged. This thing about the job was as much news to me as it was to Thomas, but as soon as I heard myself say it I knew it was true. Another part of my life gone, chunks of glacier broken off into sea ice.

"Jesus, man," Thomas said. The invective drew a sharp look from Liz, which Thomas ignored. "No wonder you're wandering the streets all night. You look like shit, by the way."

"Thanks."

"I'm serious. Hey, are you hungry?" He reached into the bag and rummaged, then came out with a foil-wrapped parcel, which he handed to Liz. She took it without comment. He dug in again. "Classic fucking American waste," he said. "But lucky us."

Liz was unwrapping the parcel. "See," she said, "Gyro Plus packs every order to go, because that's their like procedure or whatever, even though most people stay and eat there. So the pita sandwiches get double-wrapped in wax paper and then in tin foil, then they get paper-bagged. It's amazing, actually. It's like they think this shit's getting shipped across state lines or something. But what happens is people eat at the restaurant, maybe half or three quarters of their meal, and then what do they do with the leftover? Take it home? Go give it to a bum on the street? No. They wrap it back up and chuck it in the trash. So after the employees take the trash out, you find the bags that are from the dining room and bingo—feast." She smiled self-consciously, looked down at the ground then up at me, and then away again. "Not that you asked."

"It looks wet in there," I said. "Why is it wet?"

"Sodas," Thomas said. "Or water. Burst packets of ketchup, tahini spills. Condensation. All that organic matter in a sealed bag. It gets humid. But that's why this place is so great. With the way they do the packaging—I mean obviously it's fucking wasteful like I said and disgusting and they shouldn't, but they do, and all it means for us is that everything's wrapped, clean and fresh."

"But it's surrounded by all that filth. I mean, it's a *garbage* bag."

"But it's protected from all that."

"But still, the idea."

"Fuck ideas. It's food."

"Half-eaten food. There's bite marks. What about germs? It was *licked.*"

Liz cut in. "Some people cut the bitten parts off, but I don't bother."

"Me neither," said Thomas, "and I've never gotten sick from it once."

"Do you even eat the meat ones?"

"If it was a bag that smelled like it baked in the sun all day, I probably wouldn't," Liz said. "Your old friend here might"—she pointed a thumb at Thomas—"but he's a pretty big asshole, as I guess you know." Thomas was loving this; he nodded and grinned.

"But in this case," said Thomas, "that's not an issue, because Gyro Plus is open late on weekends, and this is all the stuff from last shift. It can't have been out here more than a couple of hours."———

It was charming, I thought, this rhythm they shared, apart from the grossness of what they were actually talking about. The way they finished each other's thoughts like an old married couple or a pair of middle school girls. But more than charming—it was hypnotic, practiced but not rehearsed, pat but not rote, it drew you in. I could see the broad contours of what was doubtless a thoroughly detailed and painfully earnest if not entirely consistent system of values. They clearly both believed in what they were doing. These were people, I thought, who knew who they were.

"But you still haven't answered the original question," said Thomas to me.

"Which was what?" I asked.

"Are you hungry?" said Liz, and held out the food in her hand. It was a falafel pita sandwich with all the fixings. Anyway that's what it had been. Was that what it still was? Or was it waste now? And if it was waste, did that necessarily mean it couldn't be rehabilitated—recycled, perhaps—into food again?

I took the thing from Liz and brought it close to my face for a look. There were diced tomatoes, hummus glops, tabbouleh in dry clumps, and the fried balls themselves, with their crunchy brown skins and soft green centers. I had eaten at this place, ordered this very sandwich, countless times. Liz had peeled back the foil with a surgeon's care. I'd watched her, and now I understood why she'd been so cautious. The pita was bloated, a supersaturated mush. The tahini had soaked through, sponging it. The foil gave the sandwich a coherent shape that it could no longer have maintained on its own, as it might have easily done several hours ago when it had been a hot meal. The thing in my hand was not hot, but neither did it have the thoroughgoing and authoritative chill of leftovers fished from a fridge. It was the temperature of the night itself.

Liz had taken one bite before handing it over. She had started where the long-departed diner left off. I tried to tell which exact bite had been hers, thinking that if I really was going to humor Thomas, I would at least curtail my risks by following close on the heels of his friend rather than some anonymous customer. But what was the difference? Liz was as much a stranger to me as whoever had bought this sandwich in the first place, and she was almost certainly less hygienic than that person. She and Thomas weren't merely dirty, they were unwashed. Their clothes were stiff. They stank. And I didn't know them—not her, not him. Not anymore.

"Are you sure there's enough to go around?" I asked. Thomas raised an eyebrow at me and hefted the white bag up.

"You're kidding," he said. "This'll feed the whole house for two days."

I took the biggest bite I could and stood there dumbly, chewing and being watched. It was drier than I'd thought it would be, and sucked up the moisture in my mouth. I kept chewing. It tasted okay, other than not being an especially impressive falafel sandwich, which of course, having been a customer there, was no more and no less than I already knew. No rancid aftertaste, indeed no hint at all of its having turned. The punks were right. It was fine. I swallowed.

We went back out the alley-street the way I'd come, but we crossed University instead of turning onto it. We went into the northeast part of town, up a few sleepy blocks, and only then took our left turn, around the back of El Indio, the drive-thru Mexican place that they told me had a dumpster also ripe for the picking. I nodded, as if filing this information away for later use. What could I say? We crossed Thirteenth Street, over into the northwest, the student ghetto, my neighborhood, and apparently theirs as well.

I saw the squat hulk that was Gator Glen Apartments, where I lived. It was a four-story building on a block-size plot, surrounded by single-family homes and duplexes. It was a monstrosity, I realized, a gray-white blot like a thrush in the throat of the night. I thought of the food in my refrigerator, and the beer. We could swing by, pick up what I had, and bring it all over to Thomas's, make the feast that much sweeter. But that would mean bringing them to my apartment, opening up to their judgment my sorry life. I knew what they would think of my white walls and white carpet and white counters. It was a sterile place, barely a home, and in a way I had always known that. I had moved there straight out of the dorms, and the truth was that the apartment was largely indistinct from a dorm. It had come furnished, all-inclusive. Moving there had been the beginning of my slow drift out of the world. I saw that now.

But still, the food. And if not the food, the beer. They would appreciate the beer. They were scroungers and would excuse anything on account of the beer. So maybe it was less about them than about me—not what they could accept, but what I could bear to have them know.

We walked on, and a block later turned north again. The building fell out of my sight line, and I focused on the oak limbs high overhead, crisscrossing over and under each other, so you couldn't be certain where one tree left off and another began. The whole mass swayed in the night breeze, a single solid billowing thing. I had fallen behind my new friends. I quickened my pace and caught up. It was only another block and a half before we reached their house.

The yard was dark and large, a sea of loose dirt and fallen leaves wrapping around the small house on all sides. It was a single-story cinder-block home, with flaking paint and a front porch with torn screens. I could see lights on in the living room. There was a chain-link fence with a latch gate, from which was hung a broken plank of finished wood, perhaps a former bookshelf, on which a single word had been painted in loping strokes of blue: *Fishgut*. An orange VW microbus was parked in the yard, like an island in the leaf-sea. A red extension cord snaked out one of the bus's open windows, ran clear across the yard and into a living room window that had been left open just wide enough to admit the cord. Liz opened the fence gate and held it for me. Thomas closed it behind us. I made my way up the walk, or what I believed was the walk, though all I could make out beneath my feet were more dead leaves. The front door was ajar: an inch of light. Liz swung it wide.

A pair of aging hippies were on the floor in the middle of the living room, even though there were two couches and nobody sitting on either one. A girl had her legs curled up under herself on a beat-up armchair. Her hair was the color of seawater, tucked behind her severally studded ears, though it stuck out in some places and was matted in others. She was reading a paperback book called *Omens of Millennium*. She put the book down splayed open on her knees and looked up at us. Her eyes were a warm brown, set close in her big round face. She had ruddy cheeks, a silver ring through her septum, and a smile that spread like a wonderful spill. When looking down at the book she had seemed to have a little chin roll, but it disappeared as soon as she'd tilted her head up. Though I hadn't seen her standing yet, I guessed rightly that she was three, four inches taller than me. She was wearing a white tee shirt that someone had stenciled on. Her own work, I guessed (right again, as it turned out). The stencil was a little blurry because she hadn't used fabric paint, but the work itself was finely detailed. A woman in a lacy, high-neck dress, her dark hair in a tight bun that rode low on the back of her head, appeared in profile, gazing off to the left. Underneath her, in stencil caps so crude I assumed the con-

trast must have been part of the point, it read HELEN KELLER
WAS AN ANARCHIST.

Liz approached Keller-girl and leaned in to give her a
kiss. The girl took Liz's hands in her own and pulled Liz
downward, into the armchair, so Liz had no choice but to
pull out of the embrace or else climb onto the chair herself,
which is of course to say on top of her friend, and this is what
she did. She first tried to straddle the chair, but that didn't
work so she flipped herself sideways—careful not to break
their lip lock—and splayed across the tattered upholstery of
its arms, then made a V of her body and sunk down into
perfect ease in the sitting girl's lap. The *Millennium* book
was lost in the press between them, its spine no doubt sco-
liating as they continued to squirm and kiss. Thomas had
gone straightaway to the kitchen with the food, to sort the
spoils from the spoiled, as it were. I wasn't sure what I was
supposed to be doing, and so simply stood in silence, hands
jammed in pockets, watching the kissing girls.

When the kiss finally broke, Liz looked back my way,
and the second girl's gaze followed Liz's own. "I'm Katy,"
the girl said to me.

"Hi," I said.

"You're still standing in the doorway," she said. "Aren't
you allowed in?"

"I'm Thomas's friend," I said.

"Then you must be allowed in," she said. The hippies
ignored us altogether. I entered the room. Against one wall,
a big boxy TV with its face bashed in sat on top of a coffee

table. A bouquet of papier-mâché roses sprouted out of the jagged black glass hole. Thomas came in from the kitchen. In the light I could see him clearly for the first time since we'd met in the street.

He had round black plugs in his earlobes and a ring through one eyebrow. He had a thick neck and clearly spent time working out. He was jacked, is what I mean. With his hoodie off, wearing just an A-frame shirt and black jeans, his body looked like a weapon. He had a dirty-orange Mohawk. It was wide and short on his otherwise bald head. I had been to this kid's bar mitzvah and remembered how he'd suddenly insisted that everyone stop calling him Tommy, because that was a kid's name and now he was a man.

"Dinner bell!" Thomas shouted, holding the *e* in *bell* like a town crier, and down the hallway came people in various states of undress, wakefulness, and sobriety. The living room filled with warmth and odor, bodies and nuked food, the buzz of conversation. Someone said we should put the stereo on and someone put it on, and then someone said come on, turn it up, and someone said okay, quit yer bitchin'. Noise flooded the room. I couldn't figure out who lived there and who was hanging out. Obviously it didn't much matter. I could hear beer cans cracking, and a bottle of Old Grand-Dad bourbon was making the rounds. When it came to Katy she swigged like a sailor, and Liz—still splayed in her lap—growled low in her throat and then matched her, and then they went back to tonguing. I was sitting on the floor at the foot of the arm-chair they were piled in (the couches were full now), so my neck was sort of craned back and up at them, the angle almost vertical, my body all twisted around.

Katy broke their kiss this time and whispered something in Liz's ear. Liz passed the bottle back to Katy ("Hey, no fair!" shouted someone) but she didn't drink. Instead she reached her hand down over the side of the chair: toward me. When our fingers touched around the long glass neck of the bottle, a skittering electricity passed between us. I took the bottle from her and turned my body around, so that I now rested my back against the side of the armchair, my head level with the armrests and therefore next to Liz's own head. A searching hand, Katy's, stroked Liz's hair and mine together, like we were parts of the same great lazing creature. When she raked her nails lightly across my scalp, I shut my eyes tight and told myself *don't you dare cry*. I couldn't remember the last time I had been touched at all.

"Come *on* already!" shouted someone. "It's a bottle, not a math test."

My eyes still closed, Katy's hand still in my—our—hair, I tipped my head and let the warm glass touch my lips. It was bad, bad bourbon and I had never been so glad to be anywhere. I held the bottle out and a hand took it. It went away and eventually came back, then went again and came. Katy's hand played endlessly back and forth between my hair and Liz's. It was unending movement, but belied no restlessness or wavering. It was tidal, her touch, possessed by an authority derived straight from nature, or so suggested her flittering fingertips when they brushed gently, and so insisted the full digits when they settled in for a longer moment, twining up a lock of mine, making my skin sing.

Thomas took me on a tour of Fishgut, not that there was much to show. There were three bedrooms—his, Katy's, and one outfitted with two sets of bunk beds as a guest room or travelers' rest. They were all scenes from the same low-budget disaster movie. The linoleum in the kitchen was faded past pigmentation, but held on to a kind of hazy hangover memory of having once been green. It was spattered with paint of all possible colors, smears and stripes and streaks on the cabinets, counters, walls, ceiling, even stove. There were also designs and graffiti—people's names and handprints. Dates. On the face of the fridge, a mud-colored all-seeing eye shot laserlike rainbows out from its pupil in the cardinal directions.

"Housewarming party," Thomas said.

"How long ago?" I asked.

"Six, seven months, I guess."

"Where were you before that?"

"It's a whole other story. I'll tell you sometime."

We passed through the kitchen door and out into the yard. He pulled tobacco and papers from a pouch of Drum.

"You want one?" he asked.

"I don't smoke," I said.

"That's a good boy. Your mother's proud."

There were no chairs out back, not even a porch really, just a small slab of concrete on which we stood beneath a bug light while we stared at the dark and talked.

"So how did the house get its name?" I asked.

Thomas pointed across the yard, to a pup tent in the far back corner, a small thing visible mostly in silhouette against the high wooden fence. A red Catholic prayer candle in a tall round glass was half sunk in the dirt before it, lit. I hadn't noticed this.

"Parker," Thomas said, his voice rich with disgust, like the name was bad milk in his mouth. "It's got some kick to it at least. *Fishgut.* It'd be a sweet name for a band, too—except there's already Fishbone, I guess. Still."

"A guy lives out there?" I asked. Thomas laughed nastily, I didn't think at me.

"Used to, kind of. Now just his tent does. Nobody knows where he is."

"Weird."

"Yeah."

"Well anyway, what does the name mean?"

"Stupid shit. Don't get me started. Honestly."

"And these are your friends?"

"Best friends in the world," he said. He went down to one knee and gingerly crushed out his half-smoked cigarette on the concrete slab. He stuck the butt behind his ear for later—waste not want not, I guessed, but Jesus Christ. We went back inside to rejoin the party.

What time was it? Later, late. Whatever. Who knew. The bottle was empty. Some happy punks went to smash it in the street. I didn't follow them, and the shatter did not carry over the stereo, which still blared, though nobody was paying it much attention anymore. The strike team returned and reported success. They began to hunt around for what else to smash. Others began to drift off to wherever they'd come from, out the front door or toward the various bedrooms, or else stretched themselves out on the couches if they were staying but didn't have beds or bedmates here.

Owl and Selah, the hippies, retreated to the van in the yard, which I had learned they lived in. I didn't know where Thomas was. A girl unfurled a sleeping bag from a beat-up backpack, laid it out on the hard linoleum floor, climbed in, and then rolled over so she faced the wall.

Katy stood before her own bedroom door, peering back at Liz and me, and held the position a moment, making sure we saw how she was seeing us see her. Then she took a single step into the room and winked out of our vision. In her place was the long crack between her door and the jamb, dimly shining.

"She doesn't do good nights?" I said to Liz, trying to not sound hurt, but failing and knowing I'd failed.

"You mean you're not coming?" Liz said, sounding surprised if not precisely hurt herself, at which point I only for the first time understood that the last several hours had been one long invitation.

I reached my hand out before I could doubt myself, and Liz took it. A loose grip now, not like before by the dumpster. She led me, flicking the light switch as we passed, so that darkness swept over the couches behind us, as if it were the fact of our exit that had driven the light from the room. The dim issue from Katy's bedroom seemed enormous now. Liz didn't knock, for as I was about to learn, and probably should have already figured out, it was her bedroom as well. Katy was sitting on the bed, holding a long match over the glassy O-mouth of a Catholic prayer candle, another one like the one I'd seen outside, in front of the weird tent. This one was decorated with a large sticker depicting a blue-robed, bald-pated man with a shiny, flowing beard. He had sad, know-ing gray-green eyes and held a gilt-edged volume against his breast. White letters identified him as St. Jude, Patron of Desperate Cases.

Katy touched the burning head to the wick, then pulled the long match back from the glass and blew it out even as the saint's eyes brightened, backlit now. She rose from the bed and placed the candle in a corner of her window. Through the oak-leaf ceiling over the yard we could glimpse the sky, black still but stiffening with prelight. Katy took all this in, then turned away from it and toward her bed, where we curled, waiting for her to come meet us. A week went by.

SUNDAY

Katy wakes up early, but not earlier than Liz, who is somehow always one step ahead, bright-eyed and raring, ready to proffer her body, time, attention, whatever Katy wants that Liz can give. It's a lot to handle, sometimes, to be responsible for that big a share of somebody's happiness—of the hours in another person's day. One great thing about David, he's never a step ahead of anyone. Just look at him there in the bed between them, his head turned to one side (hers), mouth hung open like a tent flap, dead to the world. His beard's coming in, a dark stubble that begins high up on his cheeks and trails off down his neck, just barely linking up with his chest hair, wisps of which reach nearly to his Adam's apple. Splayed out like he is, covers pushed down below his waist—the heat's already barely sufferable—you can see how his hair courses like a lazy river down his body: deltas into a vague eagle like a crude tattoo on his breast, then thins down his stomach, gathering again around his belly button in a whorl. From the belly button down to the nest of his pubic hair the pale skin is almost hairless, save for one wiry line down the middle, like a rope ladder flung between ships.

What time is it, anyway? A few minutes past ten. Not bad.

"We should wake him up," Katy says.

Liz thinks maybe they should let him sleep.

"Nah, come on, he'd want to go with us."

"I guess so, yeah." This is what most arguments with Liz are like. Not that *this* is an argument by any stretch. Also, when do they ever argue? What could they possibly even have to argue about? So, *conversations* then. Anyway, this is how it is with her, and there are days when all Katy wants in the world is for Liz to want anything other than whatever Katy wants. But then there are all the days between those days, aren't there? Katy smiles. Love is baffling. Isn't that the best thing about it? Top three at least.

Katy grabs the hem of the canary-yellow sheet they're sharing and with an assured flick of her wrist whips it free of the bed, exposing all of their nakedness. She leans in and takes David in her mouth, goes to work while the sheet drowses groundward, transforming the heaped clothing on the bedroom floor to some anonymous mountain range smothered in sun.

Not that she wouldn't be doing this regardless—who needs a reason to screw, after all?—but a few nights ago

when they were all really wasted, and in the sloppy process
of stumbling to bed, David got this sort of crumpled look on
his face and said he had to tell them something. Katy had
one of those moments she sometimes gets where she doubts
God's abundant and everlasting grace. For like just a flash
of a second, but still. That's another way of saying that she
thought he was going to tell them he had some fucked-up
STD. But no, it was nothing like that—more like the opposite of that, if the word *opposite* makes sense here, which
in terms of how Katy views the world, it does. David had for
some reason felt compelled to make confession. He talked
a lot about the Internet, which Katy knows nothing about;
and porn, which bores her because there's no reason to watch
something you could be doing yourself; and about an old
girlfriend, which interested her mightily—who *doesn't* like to
hear about their lovers' lovers?—and these topics seemed to
all relate, somehow, to one another as well as to a larger thesis
about how much he had hated his life, for so long, without
ever having consciously realized it until the night he met all
of them. Drunk as she was, Katy couldn't quite put all the
pieces together, though as Liz pointed out the next day, given
how drunk *he* was, it was distinctly possible that he'd left out
whatever might have been the keystone idea. The upshot,
basically, was that it was messing with his head to be living what—let's be honest—is basically every straight guy's
number one jerk-off fantasy. Part of him couldn't help but
wonder if maybe he'd lost his mind—was in some institution, dreaming all of this, as if Katy and Liz were actually

just vivid and resonant hallucinations, perhaps induced by acute pornography overdose.

The girls hadn't been sure whether that last thing was supposed to be a joke or not—or if David even knew—but Katy as usual followed her peerless instincts and took him in her arms like a mother and held him while he bawled, rocked him like a big drunk baby, and made pissy faces at Liz until she finally relented and hugged him, too. They hadn't screwed that night, only held each other, and Katy had whispered over and over again that there was nothing to be ashamed of or angry about, that everything was bound to be okay, in fact already was okay. As she spoke, Katy hoped both her lovers were hearing this message and taking it right to each heart, where it could mean unto each as each needed, world without end, amen.

But starting the very next morning, hangovers be damned, Katy began—and now, this morning, continues—a relentless campaign of fucking David, having David fuck Liz, him watching the two girls, and as often as possible all three of them in ecstatic triangles—anything Katy can come up with (and ply Liz into trying) in order to drive home the lesson she wants him to learn, which is that no light-box, no *machine*, can ever come within a country mile of the sweat-blind holy thing itself. This, *this*, is the truth and the life.

So that's the subtext to David's morning hummer. Meanwhile, somewhere behind her, Liz is between Katy's legs, making her feel perfect and loved, but Katy's trying to stay focused on David, who's awake now—she can tell it from the way he draws breath, and the fact that certain *other* parts of his body are now also beginning to stir. He says something she doesn't catch, it might in fact be not-words, a yawn. Now his searching hands have palmed her swinging tits, steadying them, pointer fingers lazily circling round her nipples. Good morning, sunshine.

Things have been nice this week, with David here. Katy hopes he stays and it seems like he's going to. He doesn't give the best head Katy's ever had, but he can hardly be blamed for not being some magical outlier in what is a fairly substantial body of statistical evidence. And to give credit where it's due, he's somewhere in the upper-middle range of the bell curve, no mean feat in itself. What he lacks in pure skill he makes up for in determination and exuberance. Truth be told, there's a way in which his earnest questing, be it hit or be it miss at any given moment, is actually *more* fun than getting it from Liz, the ace, the aficionado, who can play Katy like some video game, and bring her to the YOU WIN screen in record-setting time. Which is—whoa—basically what's happening right now. Katy's going to come in like a minute, and the gathering ache makes the world behind her closed eyes brighter, *Dear God of Earth and Heaven I thank you for the orgasm I am about to receive*, but there's this other restless part of her that can't help feeling like *home again home again, jiggety jig*—sigh.

Katy decides to see if she can get David to come at the same moment Liz makes her come. That'll be interesting, right?

About twenty-five seconds later it turns out that the answer to both questions is yes. Katy wipes her chin and collapses theatrically on top of their boy. He's breathing hard and stroking her hair. Liz lies down on her belly beside them, in the spot where Katy sleeps rather than in her own, and watches the two of them with these sort of moon eyes that Katy's worried are maybe just a little too dewy to ignore. Why doesn't Liz look as proud of herself as she usually does after making Katy come? Katy slaps her girlfriend on the behind. Playful, no pain, but the crisp rapport of the palm on the cheek says *atten-TION*. And like a bucket up from a well here's Liz back from Neverland. Two blinks and the dew is gone, her eyes lasered on Katy's, ready for instruction.

"Flip over," Katy says. "It's your turn."

"Nah," Liz says with a little shrug. "We have to get ready. We'll be late."

"We won't," Katy says. "Come *on*." Katy can feel Liz's hesitation. On the one hand, she's into the whole self-denial-as-sign-of-devotion thing. On the other, Katy obviously wants to do this for her, in the name of equality, anarchy, or just wanting to, and the prime directive of Liz's life is *whatever Katy wants*.

So she does it, flips her body over, full yield, *take me*, and tries to release herself into the feeling of being open to feeling good. David is kissing her and playing with her breasts while Katy is working on her downstairs—she loves Katy *so* much—and she's starting to breathe a little heavy. She even makes a halfhearted play for David's cock, expecting to find it limp, but it turns out he's already ready to go again. Startled, she jerks her hand back. No thanks. A few minutes later her partners switch spots, and this, actually, is much better, because even though part of her doesn't really want David inside her, at least now she's getting to kiss Katy, and hug Katy, and grab at Katy's breasts, which are bigger than hers—meaty and soft, like all of Katy; how unlike nubby, skinny tight-titted Liz—and she pulls Katy forward—*smother me with you, lover*—and pivots her pelvis so David pops out of her, and he gets the message and sticks it in Katy instead, Katy who is a blast furnace, dynamo, sun raging over and lighting up and making possible the world. Liz can feel Katy's heat, radiation and rain, the raw and blessed pleasure her girlfriend takes and produces. God is both the knower and the thing known, as well as the act of knowing that unites them, unmasks the wholeness that always already existed and exists. This is a slice of infinity made manifest, reified, captured in Katy's act of fucking and being fucked, by Liz, by David, by whoever and however many—and these thoughts elate Liz but also hurt her, in a certain sense, like in the sense of her maybe not mattering to Katy (though of course Katy always claims otherwise) or if she *does* matter, if she *is* loved, maybe it's not enough (*but what would, what could ever be enough for you, Liz, really, being in your own way as insatiable as tireless Katy?*) or even when it *is* enough and she knows it, is it enough of the *right kind* of love (*you bad anarchist, you Little-faith*) but Liz, making the most of what faith she does possess, pushes these thoughts away, forces them out, replaces them with one, one alone, singular and all-encompassing like God is, one thought that makes her infinitely happy because it is the beautiful truth (*this is what prayer is Lord she's my altar may I worship You forever*) and the beautiful truth is the thought of Katy's pleasure, and thinking these words to herself over and over— *Katy's pleasure Katy's pleasure Katy's pleasure Katy's Katy's Katy Katy*—a chant in unsprung rhythm, she blots out the chattering doubts of that demon her consciousness and there in that throbbing vacuum finds a space both limitless and impossibly close, where she is fearless and safe, prone in joy and trembling, the tremble that becomes the bodyquake, and even though she doesn't want to break her mouth away from her lover's, she simply must issue a strangled, triumphant cry through teeth gritted as if in tremendous pain.

Now here are her lovers on either side of her, kissing her closed eyes, licking tears from her cheeks, stroking her all over gently, tracing lines on her slick skin. They're all angels in Heaven; animals in some cave. Liz lets out this massive raggedy sigh. It sounds like a cartoon, she thinks, like a sound effect or something, and only now, in the moment of her hearing herself think the thought about her thought about the sigh, does she register the sad fact of her restoration to the fallen state in which she exists, her noumenal and bound existence, though this hurt is mitigated by the comforts of familiarity, *home again home again*, and isn't it sort of wonderful to pull back from the infinite, withdraw into the skimpy little cosmos of the shuttered-up self? The demon already chattering again, and this torment not without some quotient of pleasure—*Liz, you masochist, you head case*—she berates herself for ever having doubted her lover, or the fact that she's the luckiest girl in the whole wide world.

Now they're running late for church and there's still this problem of what will David wear. The plain white tee shirt he had on when he came here would be pretty much accept- able, maybe, only he can't find it. He's scouring the heaps and piles strewn about the bedroom floor, flinging one wrong item after another from his search path. Nothing. He's like a lawn mower with no catch-bag. For the past few days he's been wearing the HELEN KELLER WAS AN ANARCHIST shirt that Katy had on that night they all met. Since then, she's been wearing a sleeveless puke-green hoodie (he loves the brown shrubs of her hairy pits) and Liz only ever wears black. Ex- cept for today, apparently, when both girls are dressed up sort of like they decided to be librarians for Halloween. Well, wherever the white shirt's got off to, it's staying there. They need a backup outfit.

Katy and Liz are rummaging together in the bedroom closet, the closet door eclipsing them from David's view. They're in there long enough that he begins to wonder if they're getting up to something, and if so if he should join them—can they really be serious about this trip to church?— but then they emerge, exultant, bearing forth a man's pale pink dress shirt that looks as if it hails from some dumb movie made in the early '90s about corporate malfeasance in the mid-'80s. Where did it come from? A thrift store, an old lover, the trash—who knows? The point is it's here. Now let's see if it fits.

David buttons it up and stretches his arms out to the sides, then forward. It's baggy on him, but it'll do. There's a coffee stain like the map of a sandy island on one of the shirt-tails. He frowns at it. He's standing in front of Katy's full-length mirror, which she found by the side of the road some months ago, and which, despite a jagged forking crack like petrified lightning through its middle, is still more than adequate to their needs. David sees himself sliced and sectioned, all the angles slanting crazily and none quite adding up. Liz is behind him, a Picasso face peeking around his shoulder. She says he should tuck the shirt in to hide the stain. Also, it'll seem less puffy that way. She reaches around his waist, opens his jeans up, pushes them down his thighs (couldn't find his underwear, either, apparently), and smoothes the fabric of the shirt down all around. She pulls the jeans back up and closes them—all business—then fidgets with the fabric to make sure the row of shirt buttons lines up with the button on his jeans.

You know what? He looks okay.

And so off they go through the late morning sun, through soupy swamp air, past still-dark houses, bars with their faces veiled by metal pull-grates, toward St. Augustine Catholic Student Center on University Avenue. They slip quietly into the eleven-thirty mass, which has already begun, squeezed together in an otherwise empty pew in the dead-last row like the bad kids in class. Katy's favorite part is the recitation of the creed, which they at least haven't missed. She loves how they lay everything out in that blasé liturgical murmur, as if nothing could be more reasonable and mundane. The whole thing is teaching her something, but she isn't sure what.

David has never been to a church service before. Like really and truly: never. Not once. He's on his knees during silent prayer. The kneeler, which folds out of the pew in front of him, has got a light ocher pad that looks like leather but feels more like vinyl. He's unsure at first of whether it can bear his full weight—it looks kind of flimsy—but everyone else seems to be going for it so he does too and of course the thing holds. Relaxed now, sort of, he starts to think about how *strange* this all is, how unlikely—not his being here now but his never having been before—and what it says about the place he was brought up: something about Jews being clannish, closed off. Protective, his mother might say; and with good reason, his father would undoubtedly add. Weirdly, sitting here, he can for the first time in his life understand what it is they're so afraid of.

The priest with his shepherd's crook, or whatever you call it. Wisps of pungent smoke from the swinging censer. Mother Mary ablaze in east-facing stained glass. A boy in a white smock-thing ringing a small gold bell. And above it all, mounted high, close to the vaulted ceiling with its long wide ribs like the hull of an overturned ship, hangs the Man. He gazes down with His weary eyes, blood running from the thorn wounds in His scalp, the gash in His side. And yet His countenance is steadfast. He emanates endless love from the very heart of His endless pain.

This shit's kind of amazing.

He glances over at Katy, who has been watching him approvingly and now meets his gaze with one of her signature incomparable smiles. It's like she can't help but beam all the time. Though maybe that smile was for Liz, who is on his other side, looking over his bent neck to watch Katy watching him. But really, what's the difference? Katy is inexhaustible, she's a wellspring, her reserves don't run dry. There's enough of her for both of them. (And then some, no doubt.) He puts a hand on each of their thighs and squeezes. Not sex now, but something both deeper and more elemental: intimacy, proximity. From each girl comes an answering hand.

There they all are: look at them, on their knees, heads bowed but eyes wide open, joined. A veneration of presence, the breaking down of the walls that make each of us one and one alone. A thing that is three that is also one. Godhead. He understands now why Katy wanted for them to come here.

After mass there's a reception in St. Augustine's sunny limestone courtyard, which sits beside the—rectory, is it? Katy can never keep all the names for things straight. It's part of what she likes about Catholics, all that wonky terminology and structure. Trying to make heads or tails of it, and pick out the best parts, is like being set loose on a shopping spree.

"Rectory, right?" she stage-whispers to Liz as the three of them make their way toward a folding table set with lemonade and butter cookies on top of a white plastic tablecloth. But Liz doesn't know, and David just laughs when she asks him, as if the very idea of him being able to answer her is the best joke he's heard yet today. (In fact it is.) The tablecloth flutters and snaps in the hot, hard breeze. They stand in a tight triad, together apart in the midst of the larger gaggle, letting the happy chatter of the worshipers rise up like a fence hemming them in. The lemonade is warm, and too sweet; the butter cookies are already soft with humidity. Still. If the first rule of anarcho-mysticism is *Do what thou wilt shall be the whole of the law*, the second rule is *Whatever's not nailed down.*

Katy notices they're being eyed by a pair of student volunteers. The volunteers have white name tags on their crisp white clothing: her blouse, his polo. They glance over, then turn back to each other, then glance, then turn again. Katy feels an attack of self-consciousness, a moment of crushing doubt, like the other night. It comes from nowhere, the cold hand of despair grasping her heart.

The three of them stink to hell, their grimed bodies and clothes in this merciless sun. And their attempt at dress code, the thrift store regalia, Katy's parrot-green mop not even brushed—who are they kidding? Their best attempt at appearing civilized is basically indistinct from parody. Not their intention, of course, but try telling that to the morality squad over there. Katy shifts her weight from one leg to the other, like a kid who has to go potty. Nervousness flashes over her whole body like the cold blast that greets you at the door of a walk-in freezer. It makes her breath short. She dry-swallows her butter cookie. Her lemonade's all gone but she can't refill her glass—won't, anyway—because she knows they're watching her, all three of us, thinking how we're just dirty punks here for a free snack, freeloaders, which of course is a part of the truth, but not even close to the whole. Hell, not even the half.

She's about to announce that it's time to bolt when the student volunteers start heading over. Too late to run now that there's been eye contact. Got to deal with whatever it is. She can read the name tags now, so it's not just anyone, it's SARA and ZACHARY with the big smiles fixed to their faces. They're young, freshmen probably, or maybe he's a sopho-more. But this girl, yeesh, she's got *braces*. "Hi," she says, and puts her hand out for any of the three of them to take. Liz and David expect Katy to take the lead here, but after a long second it becomes clear she's not going to, so David reaches out and shakes hands with Sara, who beams. Liz says hello to Zachary; he nods at her.

"Welcome to St. Augustine," Sara says. "Is this your first time with us?"

"Why yes," David says. "Today's the day." Big dopey smile. Katy can't tell whether he's making fun of the girl and she doesn't get it, or if he's actually meeting her on her own level, somehow, and she's thrilled to have him there.

"Well, it's great that you've decided to join us," Sara says, addressing the empty space between David and Liz, ignoring Katy altogether, presumably because Katy declined to introduce herself. "Let me tell you a little bit about what goes on here. Are you students?" Zachary stands a few steps behind Sara, supervising or else trying to watch and learn. He could be her boss or he could be her trainee. Katy's taken a couple of steps back herself, is sort of off to one side now, adjunct to the circle but not part of it. She feels miles away. David looks at Katy—she gives him nothing—then turns back to Sara and says, yes, they're students. "Great," Sara says, her happy voice rising to a bona fide chirp. "We have all *kinds* of activities and groups for our Catholic Gators."

Katy wanted to be the one to take the hand. So why did she freeze? Not because she really thought they were going to be asked to leave—she's been here enough times to know that their whole thing is to be all-embracing. At St. Augustine they strive to break the stereotype of the church as some medieval behemoth burning the last candle for a geocentric universe. That whole thing about being thrown out was just her panic talking.

Truth is, these Catholics' moderateness, and more generally their modernity, is at the heart of what spooks her about them. How the archness and archaism of their faith seems to fit so snugly in with the regular lives they're all living right now. What can the gilded crucifix, and the Man hung thereon, mean to the boy who buys sweatshop-produced Nikes at the mall by the highway? To the girl with the sorority pin, or anyone behind the wheel of an SUV? She knows these are cliché questions, straight out of Anticapitalism 101, but cliché or not, the questions *are* earnest. How can it be that the crucified Christ means so many different things to so many different people, all at once? How can He *contain* it all?

Katy hears David and Liz thanking the two student volunteers, though all the boy did was stand there. The good-byes bring her back to earth. She sees that David now has a trifold pamphlet in his hand: *Catholic Living and Today's College Student*. They crunch up their paper cups and toss them in a blue plastic garbage can the size of an oil drum. It's about three-quarters full. They walk out of the court-yard onto University, then take the first available left off the main road. David tosses the pamphlet in a metal wastebas-ket on a corner. They're back in the student ghetto now, on oak-shaded streets lined with run-down houses filled with nonnuclear families of all varieties and kinds. Safe now from the tractor beams of the horrible good Christians, they're to-gether in a place where they can be themselves, free as the day God made them, headed home.

Their route happens to take them by David's apartment build-ing. It took a few days to get the information out of him, and when he finally told them where he lived he actually apologized. Unlike with the porno thing, a subject they haven't broached again and won't, this they took him lengthily to task on. They made him understand exactly how and why corporate real es-tate is destroying the student ghetto, and more generally, the town. That was a good exchange; by the end of it they'd had to talk him out of burning the damn complex down.

"High style," Liz says, with a nod toward the building, obviously relishing the chance to give him grief. It's basically good-natured ribbing, David knows, but still, when he thinks about his life up until a week ago—how lost and miserable he was, how he barely even understood what he was feeling—he has a hard time holding it together. The alienation from the self. The—is *ennui* the word? Soul-suffering? Despair? Since he met them, life has been one unrelenting miracle. He'd like to blot out everything before last Sunday and believe himself newborn, reborn, in a world itself newly established, exactly one week old.

"Forget it," Katy says, seeing the shadow over his face, lips pursed in the international language of *not handling this well.* "Seriously." She laughs again.

"I bet you've got all kinds of cool shit in there," Liz says. "Big-screen TV, right?"

Katy gives Liz this complex-sentence look that says, *Do me a favor and lay off him; I'll make it worth your while later.* But, interestingly, it's Liz's remark that seems to have perked David up.

"Well, it's not a big screen but—yeah, there's a TV. Other stuff, too." He pauses. There's a thought forming. They're about a half block past his building, paused on the sidewalk, Katy's hand in the space between his shoulder blades, rubbing. He's looking back at the complex. They're looking at him. He turns to them again, eyes big.

"What we need is a, like, raiding party."

They all let that hang there a second.

"Got your keys?" Liz asks.

"They're back at the house somewhere."

"Anyway, it makes more sense to come at night," Katy says.

"Why?" says Liz. "You don't have to sneak around when it's your own shit you're stealing."

So they book it back home and start digging around in the couch cushions and the piles of crap on the bedroom floor, looking for the keys. David remembers now: he slipped them out of his pocket, along with his wallet, that first night. He'd put both items on the nightstand, Liz's side, because at that point he'd known her longer. The wallet's still sitting right where he left it, but the keys are gone. Amazing to think he could live a full week of life without needing to use or even see any money, his driver's license, the keys to his own house. These people know what freedom means. He is so lucky and grateful to have been found. And sure enough here the keys are, underneath the nightstand, where they must have fallen. All the way back by the wall.

He goes out to the living room and reports success. Thomas says Owl says that if David wants, they can drive the van over to Gator Bait Apartments and load it up. It'll be easier than hauling everything by hand. "This is gonna be a riot," Thomas says. "Bunch of punks loading a whole yuppie apartment into a fucking microbus."

The raiding party is as follows: David, Liz, Owl, Thomas, and Anchor, this girl who's been coming around a lot lately. She's always wearing this one black hoodie, never mind that it's the middle of the landlocked Florida summer, hardly ever below ninety, even at night. She's a spindly five foot three, pasty-faced, broken out around her chin. She lives in the dorms, is taking summer classes, and will be a sophomore when the fall comes, that is, if she doesn't drop out like all her awesome new friends have. She's got this incredible laugh, *if* you can get her to laugh, though so far it seems that only Thomas can, which is amazing in itself given that his reputation is as the over-earnest, humorless one. But try telling that to Anchor, who's so crushed out on Thomas she'd eat glass for him, and probably wishes he'd ask her to, so she could prove it. All in all, a sweet kid.

Katy begs off the trip. "You've got plenty of hands already," she says. "I'd be getting in the way." This makes perfect sense to Owl and the rest of them—even Liz doesn't bat an eye—but David gets kind of weird. Everyone's ready to go and waiting for him, but he's pulled Katy aside. They're in the bedroom. Are things okay? Should he not be doing this? He's worried that her sitting out the raid means she doesn't really want him to live here. Or maybe Liz has said something.

"Look," Katy says. "Part of sharing your love with more than one person means needing more alone time than you would in a one-on-one monogamous relationship. It's about balance, and you'll see what I mean soon enough." She kisses him, gives him a squeeze through his jeans. "Besides," she says. "I need to spend some time getting ready for tonight. But listen: I love you, Liz loves you"—he raises his eyes a little—"come on, you know she does. She's in the van, isn't she?" As if on cue, the horn bleats in the yard. He's holding this whole thing up. "We both love you, and you love us. Now go already, so you can get your ass back here." Another hearty squeeze—it's a miracle anyone ever gets out of this bedroom—then he kisses her one last time and then he goes.

She follows him to the front porch, where Selah, on a dirty plastic patio chair, looks up from the hemp necklace she's twining to watch him pass by. David walks out to the van and climbs in the open side door. Thomas shuts it behind him. Owl, in the driver's seat, sticks his hand out the window and waves at her, a rollie between his first two fingers. Selah smiles, sending him good vibes. The cherry of his cigarette falls out, a weak streak of orange-red through the blue afternoon. It lands on the leaf carpet and smolders, but does not ignite.

Katy stands next to Selah, kneads her friend's shoulders as the two women watch the raiding party set out. The hardest part comes first—navigating the bus around the house, through the narrows of the side yard, to the back where the vehicle access gate is. "Oh," says Selah softly. Katy's still kneading, improvising a deep-tissue sort of thing. Is this the chance—finally—for her and Selah? Not that she's been nursing some secret lust all this time, but once you have your hands on somebody, isn't that just like the next obvious thing? The hippie gazes up at the punk. "Thanks," she says, wriggling free of Katy's hands. "Do you think they'll hit the liquor store on their way back?"

The bus is nosing out of the yard now, coming back up the street and passing them. "Hey guys!" Katy bellows at the bus. It jerks to a stop in the middle of the intersection at their corner. The reverse lights come on.

The raid takes about two hours. There are myriad small scores—a bedside clock, one of those little wooden handheld back massager things—but the standout plunders are the TV, the stereo, the CDs, and the pillows from David's bed. He rented the place furnished, so they can't take any of the furniture, not that they want it. What about the scanner? Well, there's no computer here to take—when they ask him, he says it broke and he never replaced it; nobody checks the tub—so what good is a scanner? Might be worth some cash, though not all that much, probably, certainly not as much as you might think if you didn't know about these things, which Owl doesn't. It was probably what, a hundred bucks new, Liz figures. Maybe less. Not that she knows, either. She's sort of a technophobe, an aspiring Luddite. She just doesn't want to deal with the thing, period. Owl, on the other hand, with typical hippie pragmatism, thinks money is money. So okay, let's say it's theoretically worth half whatever the original price was. Whom do they sell it to? A pawnshop. Would a pawnshop want computer stuff? There ought to be one out there that does; it's a growing market, after all. Yeah, but now this is starting to sound like a lot of work.

David's in his bedroom packing himself a duffel's worth of clothing, careful to leave behind anything with a prominent logo on it: Nike, A&F, Tommy. Fuck that shit. He can hear Owl and Liz arguing. Thomas, in the kitchen with Anchor, can hear them, too. Thomas has his head in the fridge. The milk's turned, but everything else is still mostly good. There'll be feasting tonight, that's for sure, plus the long-term gains in staples and condiments. All this *and* a twelve-pack. Life is grand and the Lord provides, as Katy or Liz might say.

But fuckin' A, man, those two are still going back and forth about that stupid computer thingie.

Thomas leaves the fridge door open and the twelve-pack on the kitchen table. He goes out into the living room, pushes past his quarreling friends. He knocks the scanner clean off the desk. It lands on its side on the carpet. He flips it upright with his boot then puts that same boot through its lid and face, shattering the plastic top and beneath that, the glass of the scanning bed. Problem solved.

David, still in the bedroom, hears the dull crash and then the shatter, but he doesn't stop what he's doing or even call out to ask. Given that nobody's screaming, it follows that nobody's hurt, so who cares?

Thomas walks back into the kitchen and finds Anchor sitting on the floor, chin in hands, staring at nothing.

"Hey, what's up?" he says. "You seem, like, *off* today."

"Yeah," she says, "I don't know, I didn't really sleep last night. And my period maybe."

"You're not on your period."

"No, I mean yeah, of course. I mean I think that it's coming," which is technically true since isn't your period always coming anytime you're not actually on it?

"Oh," Thomas says, hoping to convey that he's a guy who *gets* what she's going through, or gets that he *can't* get it, or whatever the thing is he's supposed to be letting her know he feels.

Anchor's not going to say this, but last night, instead of going over to Fishgut as planned, she let her dumbass roommate talk her into checking out this party that the roommate's boyfriend's frat was throwing. And there was fancy tequila there, and a bong, and it went the way these things go, and then she was somehow back in her dorm room—alone, thank God—throwing up a pizza she didn't exactly remember ordering. How pathetically bourgeois. And now here she is being a drag, barely sentient, while this amazing thing is going on in front of her. She's truly envious of David's courage. He's a role model, that's for sure. David the hero! So okay, Anchor; time to pull your shit together. Get back out there on the field. She lifts herself up off the kitchen floor by pure fiat, too quickly and so her vision swims, but she doesn't stick out a hand for balance. In fact, she doesn't let on at all. She just stands there, giving Thomas her best blank face, praying he doesn't press her any further. A few seconds later and she's recovered, is ransacking cabinets, keeping herself alert with a little fantasy about how it's gonna be when it's only her and Thomas doing this exact same kind of looting at her father and stepmom's place in Ponte Vedra Beach.

When nobody's paying attention, Liz pokes into the ruin of the scanner and finds the last of the three Polaroids, the close-up, which David apparently never bothered to put back in whatever shoe box with the other two. It's bent but not torn. She's got an idea now about what he said the other night. The big confession. What a prick, to have done this to this poor girl, doubtless without her knowing, much less consenting, and after the way she—that is, the girl, not Liz— put herself out there to please him. Men. And yet, doesn't it sort of put his whole life in a kind of instant perspective for her? *For repentance to emerge, a person first must despair with a vengeance* . . . She could pocket the picture, show it to Katy. Or she could keep it to herself, a little ace in the hole in case of—well, she can't think of an example, but that doesn't mean there won't be one. Isn't that the whole point of in-case-of? But then her fingers pause mid-reach; she feels a stirring, an upswell of something within herself, this difficult and not quite nameable emotion, one that rarely visits her and that she always associates with the way she imagines Katy feels, effortlessly, all the time. The translation by grace of rage into mercy. Is *compassion* the word?

She leaves the Polaroid where it is.

Now the van's loaded. They're pretty much ready to go. Owl, Anchor, and Thomas are in the bus; David and Liz are making one last sweep. She's looking at the block of knives on his counter. They're Henckels, which is seriously high-end cutlery. He says it was a housewarming present from his parents, or some aunt. He doesn't remember now. Anyway, he doesn't even cook. Liz was going to take them earlier, then didn't, but is now on the fence again. It's like, salvaging is very anarchist, but coveting and owning and pack-ratting are not. Point, counterpoint. So what to do?

"I guess I could always swing back by," she says, meaning if she breaks down in a day or two and wants them after all, maybe as a little self-reward for not swiping the picture. Unless of course she were to come back by for the knives, and end up grabbing both, which is also possible. The thing about compassion is it rots like fruit.

"No," David says. He doesn't raise his voice, but there's a conviction in it that startles her. He's shaking his head; weird look on his face she can't read. Or else its sad unreadable muddle is itself the message, plain as day. "Take them now if you want them. I never want to see this place again."

Oh-kay, Liz thinks, tucking the block up under her arm. He sounds so sure of himself. She wonders how long he's going to last at their house, before whatever head trip he's on runs its course. Or he gets tired of Katy, which is what always happens with these thirds they pick up, these men Katy attracts, desperate young men lost at sea in their own too-easy lives, and Katy the captain of the steamer that plucks them from the yachts they take for leaky life rafts. Which makes Liz, what, skipper or something? Or better yet, first mate? A terrible pun, and moreover: not the point. The point is that after all the succor and safe passage, the spirituality and the sexual healing and rocking each other like ocean waves, comes landfall. And when that happens, he goes. Whoever he is, whatever he might have promised to her—to them—in the heat of whatever, is forgotten or denied. He's healthy now, well rested, ready for the world again. No more need for big ideas about a God who loves you without conditions, or the way we were meant to *really* live; he's thinking about getting his old job back, maybe patching things up with Betty Sue. That's the pattern, and David fits it, though admittedly not as snugly as she's used to, which is to say, as she would like. His going nuclear on his life like this is something she's never seen before, and truth be told she actually sort of pities him. He's drunk on the discovery of how easy it is to drop out of the world. What he doesn't yet know is how fucking *hard* it's going to be to get back in, but that's because right now he believes he'll never want to. And there's no way she could explain it to him, convince him of all this—he'd only think she was trying to get rid of him—so why not make the most of the situation? In a week or a month or whatever, when he realizes the scope of his disaster, he'll probably want a lot of this shit back. So she'll return the knives to him, if and when he asks. She promises this to herself, because despite his scuzzy secret, despite herself, really, she's genuinely growing to like him, which is a lot more than she can say for some of the people Katy's brought home. And yes, she knows that she, technically, is the one who brought him into the house, her and Thomas, but that's not what she means at all. His coming into the bedroom, into their *lives*, was all Katy's doing, and it's just a fact that, like God, sometimes Katy works her will through Liz. Ah, Katy, Katy,

ks in Liz's angry armor, so
ile on her face now, a smile
, why not let him? He tries hard
all. Hell, why not kiss him? Right
the life he's immolated—this empty
glass, and these superior knives—and
al of their truce, their alliance, in the name
links them, the head of their triangle, the one
re. This kiss Katy won't witness is for that very
the ultimate testament to the depth and perfection of
devotion. Never am I more yours than when I am apart
m you, doing those things of which you will never know.

He tastes good, he holds her right, but still, the only thing
making this possible is that in her heart she knows he's only
a ghost. She's thinking ahead to the days and weeks after his
inevitable departure, when Katy will be wounded by the loss,
weakened and needful—she so rarely is—and Liz will get to
tend to her and the two of them will be in utopia for however
long. Until the cycle starts up again. The only person who
never gets tired of Katy is Liz.

They're probably getting back to the house about now, Katy
thinks. She's riding her bike up Northwest Twenty-third
Street, to Devil's Millhopper Geological State Park, which is
basically a thick ring of trees around the mouth of a hundred-
twenty-foot sinkhole on the edge of town. Or maybe technically the Millhopper is part of the next town, Micanopy,
Katy's not sure, but in any case she thinks of it—the sinkhole—

as her favorite place in all of Gainesville, outside o͏
house. Her bike is an all-black fixed-gear, brand an͏
unknown, a good-bye gift from a girl she was lovers͏
few years back, Sienna, a butch who worked at the used
shop on University and Sixth Street. Where is Sienna n͏
Katy thinks Providence, maybe. She remembers Sienna s͏
ing something about an anarchist bike collective there. Spo͏
on the frame where the black paint's flaking reveal a buried
coat of neon green. Probably the bike was owned by a student, stolen by a crackhead, and sold to the bike shop, who
repainted it, then stolen by Sienna and gifted to Katy. Cycle
of life, Katy muses, and hey, wouldn't that be a rad name for
a bike shop?

She turns left onto Northwest Eighth Avenue, a pretty
steep hill, at least by local standards. If she had a geared bike
and/or was in better shape, this could be a twenty-minute
ride. As things stand, it'll take closer to twice that long, but
no matter. More time to think is all.

Now she's riding past the first of the planet sculptures:
Pluto. This is really cool; in fact it's why she chose this route.
Some artist got a bunch of public funding to install the sun
and all the planets in a "solar walk" down this mile-long
stretch of Northwest Eighth, with all the distances between
them proportional to the real distances, at a scale of like four
billion to one. It's amazing, the spaces between the back four,
compared with how the first six are all packed in. What a
strange, mind-blowing thing outer space is. The magnitude,
cold waste between clusters of energy; this knowledge that

staggers and stuns. Hard to imagine how God's grace shines over all of it, out from it, how His presence infuses and blesses and sustains every cubic inch, every micrometer, every light year and galaxy and void. The atoms and subatoms that comprise this world, this reality, those planet statues (past Uranus now, approaching Saturn), the road below her, the trees overhead, the bike she's riding, and—of course—her. Vast black gulfs between stars and planets, between each nucleus and the electrons hurtling in their orbits. It's not a question of belief—she does believe, with her whole self—but rather one of processing power. She can comprehend these ideas, as ideas, but she can't *see* them, can't envision the fullness, the totality of the thing *as* the thing itself. What's that verse in John? She's passing Mercury, coming up on the sun statue now. The sculptures themselves are not especially impressive, but like so many other things in this world, their value is not in what they are so much as in what they represent, or better—point toward. A not grand thing may yet be a quite grand sign. Is this why God took the shape of a man? She imagines Jesus Christ, a blazing chalk outline mapped over a galaxy, ours, complete with connect-the-dots constellations. See Him drifting through the dippers, past Orion. Her Christ is not the crucified, but the resurrected Son of Man. He who lived and Lives and, Living, delivers life and life everlasting, in the form of those glimpses of the eternal that rupture our individuality, our confinement in time. He is the archetype in triumph, a man-shaped hole in existence, the eye of the needle of the world.

Blessed are they that have not seen, and yet have believed.
John 20:29. She knew she'd get it.

By the time she arrives at the Millhopper it's four o'clock, and the park is only open till five. That's okay. Since she's not driving a car, she technically doesn't have to pay the four-dollar entry fee, and the whole thing is honor system anyhow—there's nobody watching—but this is one place she likes supporting, no matter that it's government-run. She fishes around in her jeans pocket and comes up with two singles, a quarter, a dime, and, weirdly, a Canadian coin the exchange value of which she couldn't so much as venture a guess about. Oh well. She pushes the whole mess through the slot cut into the top of the wooden box, then walks her bike over to the rack and secures it with her chain and a Master lock that she expropriated from the Walmart on Thirteenth Street. Have a nice $9.95 worth of economic sanction, you union-busting sweatshop-loving fucks.

She's got the whole place to herself. Lucky! Though it's not that surprising if you think about it. Summer Sunday like this, hot as hell and twice as muggy, though it'll be cooler inside the sink, under all that tree cover, where a sweet breeze always blows. There's this wooden staircase you walk down. At the very bottom there's a viewing platform with some benches.

As per the informational placards, the Millhopper's unique formation has resulted in something like a miniature rain forest. You can find plants in the sink that you'll hardly see anywhere else around this part of Florida, which is mostly swamplands and plains. There are several small streams and tiny falls formed by rainwater. Home to a startling variety of insect life, and so on. Katy knows all this, and isn't interested anyway. She's not exactly a nature buff. What she likes about the Devil's Millhopper is the fact that from the bottom, looking up, all you can see is a round patch of sky ringed by the tops of trees that rise fifty and seventy feet up from ground level. That plus the depth of the sink means almost two hundred feet between Katy on the viewing platform (once she gets there) and the treetop crown swaying up in the blue. It's like she's standing in the cradle of life, looking straight up at the eye of Heaven, or better yet, being looked down upon by It. Or both, actually. Why not?

She also likes the legend, the story of how it got its name. That's on a placard, too; the one sign she always makes a point of reading when she visits though she's long known the tale by heart. It goes like this: Once there was an Indian princess living here, and the Devil wanted to marry her, but she wouldn't. So, being the Devil, he kidnapped her, and all the braves in her tribe went to go fight the Devil and get her back. As they were closing in on him, the Devil made the sinkhole for them to fall in, which they did, but it didn't stop them, and they started to climb out, so the Devil turned them to stone so they couldn't, which is why there's so much water coming out of the rock faces inside the sink—it's the endless weeping of the turned-to-stone braves, and they cry not for their own sad fate but for that of their princess.

The reason Katy likes this story isn't obvious. In fact, she didn't understand it herself for a long time. The Devil is the key element. At first it seems like a pretty cool Indian legend, and okay so what, but here's the thing. The story assumes the existence of a classical Christian Devil, with the capacity for action in the world. But the Indians didn't believe in any Devil, much less that one, and so you eventually realize that this *isn't* an old Indian legend, it's a white people's legend *about* Indians. And if you extrapolate further, doesn't it seem like the real "moral," beyond the just-so story aspect of how the sinkhole formed, is that if the Indians had been Christians they might have been able to better resist the black magic of the Christian Devil, and therefore might have gotten their princess back and not been turned to stone?

Talk about your cultural imperialism; talk about plain old fucked-up. And yet. There's something beautiful about it also, sort of running concurrently with the monstrosity. She can't put her finger on it exactly, but it has to do with ideological miscegenation, how all cultures are just hodgepodges, collages, patch jobs. Try putting it this way: the monstrosity *is* the beauty.

Katy's about halfway down the staircase, a series of steep flights linked by switchback landings. She's paused on one of these, surveying all she sees before her: trying as always to really and truly *open* her eyes, heart, and spirit to this experience. Her self-articulated goal is to *take everything in*. She's even breathing deeply, gulping swollen lungfuls of wet air and holding them until the wonderful burning in her chest lets her know she's absorbed every last whisper of oxygen. May the air she releases be pure carbon dioxide; let it be as a blessing to the trees.

If you stuck the Statue of Liberty in the Devil's Mill-hopper, only its torch would stick out. (That's not counting the base, but still.) The vibe here is ancient and wild, soul-memory stirred in deep time. Primeval, if that's not too cheesy to say—and shit, Katy thinks, if it is then so what? Look around. Positively Precambrian. It's Edenic—no, no, scratch the adjective form; this is Eden. Everywhere she looks: life! Live oaks and longleaf pines. Berry bushes buzzing with attendant insects, countless ferns, plus a plenitude of lesser scrubs, shrubs, and grasses, all nameless—at least to Katy—but what do names matter? Everywhere they rise up from the soaked brown ground. Lichens blooming wintergreen-pale on trunks and branches. Arm-thick vines strung tree to tree like power lines. Who can say where they start or end? Who says they ever do? Water burbling through stream beds, or spinning free from fissured rock face into space, falling and then splashing down, sucked up with eager, greedless relish by the soil and porous lime. She's not deep enough down yet to see the Indians' tears but she can hear their burbling, can picture the vermilion mosses coating the wet black faces of stone. Spindly limbs hang low over the stair path; tiny spiders swing on threads of sticky silk so thin they're invisible until they catch the light. And lizards on the topsides of those same branches, flashing fiery speckled dewlaps, ready to mate. Squirrels giving chase up and down trunks broad and gnarled and impossible with age, and the rodents' chittering lost in the high chorus of a million cicadas, and this ceaseless noise pierced by bird squalls or some lone woodpecker's sporadic tattoo.

Everything throbbing together, and all of it holy—each single thing, and the unity of all things, and the throb itself.

Katy rushes the rest of the way down the stair path. At the bottom, on the bench, she slings her backpack off, unzips it, scrambling for her journal and pen. Got to get this all down while it's fresh. Before the ecstasy of God's abundant grace—always present, always boundless, but only ever revealed in fragments, in glimpses—starts to fade. She's flipping past unsent letters, poems in progress, sketches of Liz. It's mere seconds till she arrives at the blank page, cracks the spine of the journal for luck, sets it down in her lap, uncaps the pen, and sets nib to paper, but she can already feel the revelation draining out of herself. Trying to focus her mind, trying to snatch shreds of it back, only makes it fade faster. Why does she keep doing this? There are things that exist beyond the limit of what can be described, captured, written, or even communicated. They can only be experienced, it seems, and all the mystics she's ever read are in agreement on this one point. Does she really think she can succeed where Ibn Arabi, Isaac Luria, Aquinas, Crowley, and the anonymous monk who wrote *Cloud of Unknowing* all failed?

She puts the journal away and just sits there, a little pissed at herself but still more or less enchanted with the beauty of the place, etc. A few minutes go by, then she gets the journal back out, just to doodle or whatever. She draws a black widow, a rose, and on its own page, the A for anarchy inscribed in a heart shot through with an arrow that is also the crossbar of the A: Parker's symbol, and the unofficial "logo" for their group of friends.

It's getting on toward the time when the park closes. Probably she could stay if she wanted to—is the ranger really going to come all the way down here and check that it's empty?—but it'll be a long ride home, and there's people coming tonight, and her still without anything to say to them. Plus she's curious what happened with David and the raiding party. Better then that she doesn't dawdle. She puts the journal and pen away, starts back up the stairs. It's always such a drag having to leave this place.

It's a few minutes before six and the living room is filled with the salvage of David's life. Everyone's sitting around on the floor, picking out what they want, or what's salable. Liz is methodically checking the backs of about four hundred CDs for scratch marks. Open the case, pop the disc out, hold it to the light, put it back in the case, decide which pile it goes in. Katy enters, a sweaty mess. She's tired from her ride, plus sapped by the heat of the day, so she gives perfunctory kisses to her girlfriend and her boyfriend then makes for the shower, which is in Fishgut's only bathroom, which is at the head of the small hallway and shares a wall with the kitchen.

When she's done she dries herself off with one of the four or five towels crammed on the rack, a royal blue one, fixes it around her waist, walks topless into the living room and announces that she's taking a nap, if that's cool with everyone. Anchor, supine on the couch, peeks out through the keyhole in the hoodie drawn tight over her face. "Huh?" she says, in this totally cute voice, like a puppy yawning.

"Aw, honey," Katy coos. "What did you *do* last night?" Anchor shrugs. "Honey, why don't you come lay down in a real bed?"

Without a word, Anchor negotiates herself up off the couch and sort of gingerly stumbles between the stacks of CDs, past Katy, and straight into the bedroom. Thomas and Liz, meanwhile, are sharing a look about five pages long. It amazes Thomas—not Katy's audacity, which he's long since accustomed himself to, but the weird way in which he and Liz are allies. If any of this registers with David, he doesn't let on. Katy, of course, catches all of it, but she honestly just wants to curl up with Anchor and sleep—she's in her nurse mother mode now—not that she's going to explain herself to these two, and furthermore, not that it would be any of either of their business if she did have her mind on the other thing. Let them wallow in their negative energy, if that's what suits them; we're all freemen and freewomen here. "So okay," she says to whoever's listening, presumably David, though Selah—on the opposite couch from where Anchor was, at work on a new hemp necklace—might be giving her half an ear. "Somebody wake us in like, an hour and a half."

In the bedroom, she takes the towel off, gives herself a once-more-over with it, then lets it fall to the floor. She climbs into bed naked and sidles up against fully clothed Anchor, who will be the little spoon. The women drift to sleep, together, almost immediately, and find themselves still together in a dream where they're both standing—more like floating, actually—in some directionless, depthless, pitch-dark nowhere.

"Are you okay?" Katy asks.

"Yeah, I think so," Anchor says. Katy reaches out through the nothing and squeezes her friend's hand.

A faint light appears in the ungaugeable distance. Or has it been there and they're only now noticing? And what *is* that small bright thing that wobbles but does not waver? It's like a pinprick in a sheet at first, but then it's more like a small coin. Before, Katy felt like they were steady, or at a mild drift, and thought that the dark was water or it was space or it was solid—that it held them, in any case. Only now does she realize, in the moment that she thinks to herself that they *could* start running (or is it in fact the moment before she thinks it? or is it in fact the moment after, as if wanting made it so?)—only now does she realize that they are not afloat, nor suspended, nor buoyant at all, but rather standing on warm ground.

Anchor squeezes back and Katy knows they understand each other. They release hands and start to run.

How long have they been running for? Anchor doesn't know. She doesn't get winded easily, and running in this world is so much easier than running in the other—the one she knows is *her* world, i.e., the *real* one—even though right now she can't exactly picture it. From where she's presently at, actual life is as hazy and scattered a memory as the last hour of last night's dumb party. Right now it's like only this running is real. She can feel sweat beads forming at her hairline. She could run forever, she thinks. The light doesn't get closer or farther away. It doesn't flicker or change again.

The laws of this place operate—and she's sure that there *are* laws here—in a way that Anchor cannot grasp. But she's got an inkling that she trusts: this world may be a dream, but the ground isn't. It is real. Maybe it wasn't before but now it is. It's getting more real, in fact. Not just dirt now; sometimes the crunch of a leaf, and dull bursts of pain when she comes down hard on a small rock. She has no shoes on and is pretty sure Katy doesn't, either. She thinks they're in some kind of forest. She worries: What if there's a hole or something? What about animals? What if one of them slams into a tree? Oh, but the trees all seem to be far from them. They are dim shapes. She sees them coming and skirts them easily. She does not, of course, stop running, or take her eyes off the light. Somewhere behind her Katy is wheezing and puffing, struggling to keep up with her faster, fitter friend.

What made her think this was a forest? It's not anymore, if it ever was. Those trees, or those shapes she thought were trees, are gone now, replaced by shrubs and outcroppings of rock. The ground is different, too. The dirt is getting sandier, soon will *be* sand. There are hills in the close distance, mountains farther off. Desert again? She still doesn't know much about where they are, the world is still mostly shadow, but she knows this: the forest has given way to the valley.

So the obvious question is: where does the valley go?

On and on they run, and she can feel it in her lungs now. The air has a crispness to it, a chilly bite. Her legs are getting tired: thigh muscles, calves. So there *are* limits, even in this world. And so how must Katy be feeling? When she next steps down, Anchor's feet plunge into wet sand. She keeps her eye on the dime of brightness that sits so low on the horizon, as if balanced on that thin dark line. Is it alone the thing that lights this place up—what meager, miserly light that there is? What's that sound she hears? That rushing. That crash that repeats and repeats, instances of crash and rush running into one another, becoming indistinct auditory mush: an unending roar.

The salt in the air makes Katy feel alert. Her legs are screaming for mercy; her lungs are tied in bows. This night feels as if it's lasted a thousand years already. It may last another, could keep going on and on. Or it may end quite suddenly. Either—any—way would make sense. There will be some confusion and then they'll be—well, somewhere familiar. Wherever they were before here. She can't remember it just now, but she knows it was somewhere, and furthermore that they'll know it when they see it, i.e., when they get back. Katy's certain. But here they need to focus, because dream or no dream, whether time is short or long, they have run out of land, are inside of the tide line, down in the runny stuff, where pools gather and fill with colorful inchfish that wash in to feed and then back out again, tiny aquaverses existing for mere seconds, lifetimes on lifetimes, obliteration and rebirth.

Katy stumbles. One arm flails, wild. She goes to her knees, which sink in. Waves wash water over her legs.

Though the sea is frigid, positively North Pacific, she reaches down with cupped hands and draws some up. She points her face up at the dark empty sky, closes her eyes and spills ocean down upon herself. There's no explaining how good this feels, even though the water is incredibly salty—so salty it burns. Merely closing her eyes wasn't quite enough; she should have *squeezed* them shut. But she brings the cup of her hands back down to the water. Again. Again.

A bigger wave sweeps in and she's knocked nearly over. The waves are getting bigger all the time now. Perhaps a storm is coming. And again as if thinking made it so, there's a rumble of thunder. She looks around for lightning but sees nothing: no flash in the distance, no cloud-muted jag. Maybe she only imagined the thunder, but better to be safe. She stands up and walks out of the water, up the beach.

On a dune, Anchor is sitting cross-legged, the way that when she was a kid her teachers used to call Indian-style, holding a leather-bound book about the size of an encyclopedia volume for a second-rate letter, maybe *K*. She hasn't opened it yet. The book has no writing on its front, back, or spine. It is shut with a metal clasp—brass, she thinks—but instead of a lock on the clasp there's a button in the shape of a heart. She's pressing it but it's stuck and won't budge. She looks up and sees Katy approaching, back from whatever it was she was doing down at the water's edge. She's glad to see her friend, and stands up in greeting.

"Maybe you'll have better luck," she says. Katy shrugs, gives her this weird wan smile, takes the book. She presses the heart-button and it pops right open—of course. This is fairy princess spirit mother pagan priestess *Katy* we're talking about here. Who else should the enchanted book open for?

"What does it say?" Anchor asks, but Katy either doesn't hear her or can't answer; maybe can't make words. It is brightening in night beach world, as if the moon had risen, and indeed it has. That dime light in the distance—she'd forgotten all about it, they both had—is centered in the sky now, larger by several orders of magnitude and blazing like an oculus at noon. It's the brightest moon that Anchor's ever seen. It burns her eyes even to glance. She looks away, back down at Katy, who is still staring at the book, though not, Anchor notices, turning pages. She walks around Katy and peers over her shoulder.

There are no pages in the book. It's an unbroken surface, the inside, with no gutter in the middle, no valley where leaf curves in to spine. The inside of the book is a mirror.

When Anchor's face enters the image in the mirror, Katy's trance or whatever is broken. How long was she staring at herself like that? She snaps the book closed, holds the volume close against her body, and looks up at the moon, a disc of clean white fire, waxing huge. She feels Anchor draw close up beside her, afraid. The moon looks, Katy thinks, like the widening mouth of a tunnel, but she knows that what she sees is not an empty space, but rather a solid object or even a living thing. And of course they're not approaching it—they're not moving. It is the moon that moves, screaming silent down to greet them with its radiant kiss.

Anchor, bolt upright in the bed, crying: What the fuck oh my God Jesus fuck.

Katy, sleepily: What? Hey, don't take His name—

Anchor, screaming: Fuck you what the fuck was that?

Thomas, kicking the unlocked door open: Katy, what did you fucking do to her?

Katy: I didn't *do* anything. We had a dream.

Anchor: Shut up.

Katy: The same dream—right?

Anchor: What the fuck.

Liz, trying to get past Thomas, but failing: Katy, are you okay?

David, casually, from the living room: Hey, what's going on?

Katy, to Anchor: We were there together.

Anchor: I, I—

Katy: And so you must know the same thing I know now.

Thomas: Katy, leave her the fuck alone.

Anchor, to Thomas: Hey, dude, you're not my fucking *father*, okay?

Thomas: I just—

Anchor: No.

Liz: Thomas, let me through.

Thomas, hands in the air: You know what? Fuck every last one of you.

Liz, passing through the door space vacated by Thomas: Katy, are you okay?

Katy: I'm amazing. We both are.

Anchor, voice shaking: That was *so* fucked.

Katy, taking Anchor's hands in her own: It's okay. I know it's scary, but it's not a bad thing.

Liz, whining: What are you guys *talking* about?

David, from the living room: Everything cool in there?

Liz, to David: *Fuck you.*

Liz, to Katy: Baby, can you please let me in?

Katy: I'm sorry, but it's up to Anchor.

Anchor: Fuck it. Let's go look and see.

Here they come from the bedroom in a gosling line, Anchor out front, Liz behind her like a warden, and Katy—dressed now—behind Liz. David joins the procession and follows them out back.

(On the front porch, Owl and Selah are doing their best to pretend that none of whatever this is is actually happening, while Thomas, furious, has locked himself in his bedroom with the stereo cranked all the way up. Maybe this Propagandhi record will just blot everything out until he's capable of dealing with his friends and/or lover without wanting to punch all their faces in. He punches the wall instead, which seems like it ought to be cathartic but isn't, and now his fucking knuckles are bleeding.)

David and Liz have unstaked Parker's tent and are dragging it off its plot of ground, trying to jostle as few of the items inside as possible in the process. Anchor is directing them in their work, her eyes growing wide as the newly exposed rectangle of earth is revealed to contain a small dark square that at some point was dug up and then refilled. "Fuck me," she says, awestruck. The fear and anger that accompanied her awaking are apparently in recession now, or are maybe even gone. Her tears are dry. She looks excited, expectant, pumped.

"Should I look for a shovel?" Katy asks. "I don't know if we have one."

"I think we can do it with our hands," Anchor says. "Shouldn't be hard for all of us. It's not in deep." Katy is proud of the conviction in Anchor's voice. They awoke from their vision both knowing this, and each knowing the other knew it, but Katy feels that she can't be the one to lead here, so it really is all up to Anchor. She's the key.

The four of them go to their knees around the patch and start to dig in the loose dirt. It doesn't take long before they hit it. Liz's fingers touch down on takeout bag plastic—they all hear it crinkle—and she digs a few more handfuls out, then grabs the bag and pulls. The bag is white and says THANK YOU 24 HOURS on it in red, with smiley face wingdings flanking the declaration on both sides. Its handles have been tied together to seal it off, keep the dirt and bugs and rain out. Liz does not attempt the knot at the top of the bag; she tears through the plastic. (This causes Katy to suck breath sharply in—she herself would have taken pains to preserve the artifact.) Inside the bag is a Mead composition notebook with a black-and-white marble cover. On the part where you're supposed to write your name and what class you're in, there's a purple-Sharpie'd doodle. The A-inscribed arrow-shot heart they all know so well. Parker's mark.

See them now on their knees in the leaves, dirt under their fingernails and racing eyes aglow, scalp-tickling sweat, bodies bunched in the tightest cluster, passing the revealed testament of their prophet from hand to urgent hand. Every moment of being is an apocalypse. Every instant the world is made anew.

SUNDAY NIGHT

Here's Thomas, right hand wrapped tight in a vodka-soaked paper towel. He holds it in his clenched fist, fast against his bloody knuckles, which shriek with the cleansing sting and turn the towel pink. He walks out the front door. It slams behind him. Then off the porch, whose screen door is hung at a broken-elbow angle by a single distressed hinge. Then down the walk, past the orange VW (Owl, lounging inside, says, "heya, brother," but is ignored), and out the front fence and straight into the street. He crosses the street, the planting strip, and the opposite sidewalk, then up into the yard of the house there. There are lights on in the house, but the shades are drawn, and anyway it's not like he's up to something. All he wants is a little perspective. He walks as close to the neighbors' house as he dares, then turns around to face Fishgut. He's trying to pretend that he is somebody—anybody—else.

The first thing is that it's small. He'd forgotten that. Strange to say—after all, he *lives* there—but who doesn't know that sometimes the truth is strange? With people always coming and going, and new chapters in the grand anarcho-soap of everyone's hookups and alliances and ideologies ever being written and rewritten, it only makes sense that the place would grow outsize in his mind. Whole worlds rush up against each other in there, colliding in dark heat, or else separated by mere thin inches of concrete—not quite thin enough to punch through, as it turns out, but still, from the inside: epic. From even this minimal distance, however, this notion of magnitude is exposed for a fiction, a delusion if not an outright fraud. From the neutral zone of the across-the-road neighbors' yard, the approximate view from these proximal strangers' front window, you don't see any of the things that make this place enormous to him. All you see is a small house, poorly kept up, set back on a decent piece of land—decent for in town, that is—enclosed by a chain-link fence that the twining leaves and limbs of bushes and nuisance plants have rendered basically opaque. The most visible part of the place is its low-rise roof, gravel-coated asphalt shingles dull beneath dunes of dried leaves. They gather like so much sand or snow in the valley where the main roof joins with the little one over the porch. During the day, sunlight streaming down through the oak canopy does this dappling, idyllic thing, but now, with sunset raging full bore, the trees cast long shadows eerie in their clarity on the roof faces. This only lasts a little while, magic hour, here and gone almost as soon as you realize, like Anchor poking her head out the front door, looking to see if someone is out on the porch (*you, it's you she's looking for*) and not finding him. She appears like a mirage in the break in the green, through the triple opening of fence gate, gaping porch mouth, and front door. So why doesn't she see him, if he really is the one she's after? Because even though the sight line between them is as clear and straight as a bowling lane, he's beyond the edge of their universe, and hence not anywhere that Anchor would ever look. And now she's turning in again—going and gone. So too the sunset. Dusk is come, the bright sky gone to lead. There's a firefly rambling by the van now, an icky sports-drink green he can't quite believe is natural, pulsing off-on-off, a lazy beacon adrift in smokelight.

He crosses the street again, shuts the gate behind himself. He's home.

Thomas and Katy met through Parker, originally. This was back in '97, when Thomas was freshly dropped out. Parker had been living in a big punk rock flophouse called the Palace of Zinn. Ah, punks and their puns. That house was a disaster. It was a bad scene. Everyone was an activist, and their various prized causes drove wedges left and right. There was a slight problem with herpes there, and a larger one with methadone. The place was run by consensus, of which there was almost none. Among all this black chaos and nihilistic disarray, it seemed that there was just enough solidarity left to unite the whole house against Parker, because he didn't share their drugs or his body (neither took nor offered; neither gave nor received) and plus there was his spiritual tendency, which was almost certainly anti-anarchistic, they said, and anyway it wigged everyone out. They drove him from his house like Joseph Smith from Missouri. He was expelled by unanimous vote, himself abstaining.

During this same time, Parker and his new friends, Thomas and Katy, who liked him just fine and anyway thought the Palace of Zinn scene was busted beyond repair, were all regularly partying together in this warehouse squat by the train tracks that an old punk named Rooster had opened up and nicknamed—wait for it—the Coop.

Thomas knows that Parker looked up to Rooster—he'd been *around*, man; he was nearly forty—but he doesn't know what Rooster thought of Parker, or of any of them, other than that it was cool if they came around to hang out as long as they brought beer along, and maybe some food. Then one day Rooster said he had decided to go hook back up with his ex, who supposedly had their two kids somewhere in Indiana. Or was it Illinois? Thomas doesn't remember now, but it doesn't matter. Christ, the idea of Rooster with kids! Anyway, the old bird flew the Coop, and just like that the place was theirs.

It was during this transitional moment that they met Liz. She was a scrungy kid, maybe eighteen (maybe not quite), an ACR—Alachua County Resident; a townie—who hung out at Clasen's, the combination punk venue slash indie record store slash vegetarian burrito place that was and still is the epicenter of the local scene (now more than ever, since the Covered Dish is out of business). Thomas works off and on at Clasen's, as a cashier slash bouncer slash sound guy— whatever the occasion happens to call for on those weeks when he happens to feel like being employed. But Liz never lived at the warehouse; she just hung out. The actual chickens in the Coop were Parker, Katy, Thomas, and a junkie named Drake, another exile from the Palace of Zinn, who had been part of the anti-Parker voting bloc, but now begged for mercy. Parker gave it to him.

Parker was raised in religion. Thomas knows that much. He ran away from home as a teenager, from some fucked sect of—what were they? Snake-handlers, Adventists, Baptists, speakers-in-tongues, Witnesses, maybe renegade Mormons; no way to be sure. He was long unchurched by the time Thomas met him, but the language, the forms of thought were stuck fast. They were who he was. Parker was a big-*b* Believer, he had a God-entranced vision of all things, but because of how Thomas grew up—secular atheist Jew, same as David—the very idea of belief was foreign to him, and he did not for a long time comprehend what it was he was dealing with.

Thomas fashions himself a rationalist and, increasingly, a materialist as well. He believes in direct action, at whatever order of magnitude we're talking—from the forcible liberation of the global working class on down to some brick through a cop car window in the anonymous night. He reasons: how is the state ever going to wither away if we don't ever get around to pulling its roots up, salting the earth in which it grows? To him, a Marxist is just an anarchist who's forgotten the third tenet of his own revolutionary program. He learned this from Parker, who at one time was true black and red: a master thief, filthy as a snot rag, yet able to disappear completely at will. Thomas used to swear that the guy could melt into a concrete wall. He taught Thomas everything he knew about expropriation and evasion, which are other ways of saying survival (he said)—as well as how to hop trains.

The mystical stuff, the baffling Christ babble, was the one thing about Parker that Thomas was never able to comprehend—hell, could barely stomach—and from the beginning it was a wrench in the gears of their friendship. But he had the ugly example of the Palace punks to remind him of the constant dangers of prejudice, a closed mind, etc. Those miserable fuckers had really hurt his friend, who had only ever wanted one thing, which was to extend the concept of absolute freedom to include the free self's freedom to explore faith free of oppression. What Parker objected to was throwing the whole notion of the spiritual out with the rancid bathwater of power's general tendency to co-opt religion. Thomas didn't agree, really, but he understood where his friend was coming from, and he furthermore recognized that his own position had—and ought to have—no bearing on Parker's. That's the beauty of anarchism, of anarchy. And that's another way of saying that for Thomas, as long as Parker kept that shit to himself, which for a long time he did, the two of them got on like the brothers neither of them had ever had. Or like Thomas never had, anyway. Who can say what Parker's family might or might not have been?

One day the two of them woke up with an itch for travel, so they packed their backpacks with dumpstered bagels and gallon jugs of water, and kissed sleepy Katy good-bye. She didn't mind them having a little boys' time; she wouldn't stay lonely long. Parker and Thomas wandered out to the tracks through a warm sunrise drizzle and caught the first thing that came their way. They'd thought they were headed for South Florida, Miami Beach, maybe a little visit to Thomas's parents' place if their supplies ran low. Instead they spent ten hours in the skull-numbing shake of the dark boxcar, and clambered out at their first opportunity into what turned out to be the Philadelphia yards. They spent a week there, swimming in Wissahickon Creek—slimy, and the banks needle-strewn, but gorgeous anyway—and sleeping in a dry culvert they found. They dumpstered expired feasts from the Safeway, snuck in to see Hot Water Music play the Electric Factory, and made their beer money from receipt scams at Walmart, or by stealing coffee-table books from one Barnes & Noble and then returning them at another. They were invisible, invincible outlaw princes; wild children, lost boys. To this day, it's one of Thomas's happiest memories. Sometimes he wonders what made them hitch back to Gainesville. Couldn't they have just gone on?

But Parker hungered for visions and trials, and there were limits on his ability to resist this urge. After Philly, he began to go off more frequently, but never again with Thomas. He sent himself alone on soul errands, into the woods now, and spoke vaguely of his travels as quests, though it was never clear what it was he quested for. Thomas nursed the hurt of rejection and consoled himself with the knowledge that, his more bizarre quips notwithstanding, Parker was still in open rebellion against the established church—every last one of them, whatever the denomination. That was good enough for Thomas, pretty much. Out there in the Coop, they led noble, satisfied lives of monkish poverty cut with the finest excesses a college town affords. But Parker's troubled spirit was ever more difficult to ignore. He was both restive and inward-looking, and no longer wanted to go to shows or even get drunk. He allowed himself nothing but the various books he stole and all the time in the world to read them. He re-read, highlighted, underlined, folded corners down, made marginal notes.

The more Parker contemplated, meditated, delved within, the less interested he became in tearing down—much less forging a humane alternative to—the capitalist-imperialist system, the lie of the American dream, or anything lasting at all. All around them he saw things crumbling, as computers translated the foundational aspects of reality—distance, presence—into illusions of themselves, even as Marx had written that all that is solid melts into air. Parker believed every new technology brought about a new kind of disaster, and therefore some critical mass or terminal velocity was inevitably bound to be reached. It was the age of Late Capital; the core was rotten; the sickness was in the blood. He dreamed of entropy, but he dreamed awake. The world was hastening its own end, and he would welcome that ecstatic unraveling when it came, but in the meantime he would have them be utopians, stand apart insofar as they were able, and push themselves always farther, further away.

Thomas already understood the basics: the capitalist war machine controls the world; voting changes nothing; democracy is a joke they keep playing on us, like the gym class bully who steals your underwear then dangles it above your head, just higher than you can reach. He knew—they *all* knew— that it didn't matter which Republicrat you voted for, but Parker saw no more purpose in protest marches, peace group meetings, or whatever the campus left was hot and bothered about lately. Palestine, sexism, Greek-system domination of the student senate, union rights, Iraq sanctions, university contracts with weapons developers, or worse yet, with Nike—it would all come and go. They already lived outside capitalism's kingdom, in the gutter that ran along the base of its fortified wall, not beyond but below the field of its vision— except of course when they got caught stealing, but they were pretty ace thieves by this point. We might be trapped *in* this fucked, fallen world, Parker said, but that is not the same as being *of* it. They were strangers passing through alien land. When Katy and Thomas professed themselves anarchists, Parker insisted that this meant they were already Christians, for in his mind the two were cut from the same cloth and together formed a single shining garment, the armor of faith.

These were the teachings Thomas rejected, and which Katy adopted with her whole heart.

The reason they live at Fishgut is Drake the junkie. He was essentially Parker's first congregant, even before Katy. Drake was eager to pay back Parker's kindness, besides which it didn't take a whole lot of effort to shoot himself up and listen for however long until he nodded off. But then he went and OD'd. Wastoid. Moron. Sellout. He died right there in the Coop. Parker himself found the body: eyes open, residual warmth. And this of course brought the cops down, scattering the family to the winds.

Katy stayed with Liz at Liz's mom's place, under the pretext of being just another local girl with a home life approximately as fucked-up as Liz's own. Thomas meanwhile crashed on couches, here and there, or in the back room at Clasen's, on nights he worked closing shift. Parker stole a pup tent—the very one that stands in the yard today—from a high-end sporting goods store down Thirteenth Street. Then he fled to the woods. He lived somewhere in or near the Paynes Prairie nature preserve, but they never knew exactly. He wouldn't show anyone.

All their situations were untenable, and several recon missions in search of fresh squats had come up empty, and living with Liz's mom was driving both girls crazy (here they were, living together, and yet still having to sneak around), so they pooled their scrimpings and found this place. A small but necessary compromise of their values: to actually pay rent.

The landlord's a local. Jim Stuckins. Does it get more Gainesville than that? He actually grew up in this house and owns it outright, along with three or four other places he's picked up over the years. He hates how the realty companies level whole neighborhoods, then replace them with white-washed buildings with stupid-ass names like Looking Glass, Nantucket Walk, and of course David's own Gator Glen. A company had been picking up houses on the block. The plan was—perpetual plan is—get ahold of all of them, then level, then rebuild. Make it like that Pete Seeger song about the little boxes, only these would be shoe boxes, stacked in rows. "Die before I sell to them sonsabitches," Stuckins told them, and that was good enough for Thomas.

Stuckins is a self-described libertarian, basically an anarchist from the other direction, though of course if Thomas ever said that to him he'd probably be answered with a boot to the head. (Nobody likes to hear the truth about themselves. Didn't Jesus say that?) The rent's low, almost stupid-low, and they pay it in cash, at Stuckins's request, which is good because most of them don't have checking accounts. Thomas used to, but he's pretty sure it automatically closed after he drained it. Plus the cash thing makes Thomas think ole Jim's a tax cheat, which he respects for all the obvious reasons. These were the terms of their agreement: "Money shows up in my mail every month, you'll never see me over your house, less you call me 'cause something broke. It ever stops showing up is fine too, but then just don't be in there when I get there." In sum, renting this house is about as humane and nonexploitative as any transaction possibly could be while still taking place within the context of a capitalist mercantile exchange. It was, naturally, a handshake deal.

And of *course* Katy took this whole arrangement, when it was offered to them, as a miracle. Quote unquote.

Right when they got the house, Parker reappeared in town. Miracles sure were in ready supply that week. It was the first time in months that any of them had seen him. Something had changed—happened or failed to happen—out there in the woods. Thomas didn't know what that thing might have been, he wasn't sure that he would want to know, but he was sure that something had. Parker was different now, closed-off, distant, and genuinely spooky. His head was often cocked to one side, like he was trying to listen to fairly complicated directions being whispered to him by someone none of the rest of them could see.

It was over Thomas's considerable objection that Katy offered Parker his own bedroom in the house. Since there were three of them splitting the rent, and Katy and Liz were sharing a bed, the idea had been that the third room would stay open, for an art studio or a practice room for the band they were always talking about starting, or a crash space for traveling kids. Whatever else they could think of. But Katy broke unilaterally with the consensus, an absolute betrayal, and she did it even though she knew that Parker had no money, and that that state of affairs would never change. She was prepared to take on his burden, though she herself was borrowing money from Liz, who had gotten it from her mother, who had given her daughter $387 as a moving present, then announced herself tapped out. Katy thought God would see them through, and of course it's pointless to argue with anyone whose side God is on—though Thomas had been more than willing to give it his level best—but it turned out not to matter anyway, because Parker didn't want to come.

Katy begged him. They were at Clasen's, Thomas was working, and she'd already strained Parker's patience by bringing him here. Thomas watched them go back and forth for nearly an hour, thankful he couldn't hear a word either one was saying. Eventually Parker relented and agreed to go with her, but when they got to the property he wouldn't set foot inside.

He never left any evidence of his campsite when he wasn't actually in it—security culture, he said—so he had the tent with him, in his backpack, when he came over. He set it up in the yard, as far away from the house as he could stake it. Then he christened the house after the site of Jonah's perdition, a rebuke that could hardly have been lost on Katy, but it had been her bright idea to give him the honor of blessing the place with a name. Thomas thought, personally, that as far as names went, "Fishgut" was a pretty good one, and he liked to think that they'd all learned a valuable lesson about playing with fire and getting burned. Heartbroken, but unflinching in her loyalty, Katy herself painted and hung the sign.

Then, on the morning of the third day, they found the tent flap open, the tent itself abandoned. He was gone.

That was seven months ago. Where he went, and why, remains a matter of contention between Katy and Thomas. They agree that Parker must have reached a critical juncture in his spiritual development. He's a true knight of faith now, Katy says, a full-sprung saint. She believes he's left the tent here as a covenant of his promise to return to them. In the meantime, she's filled the tent with all the glass husks of her prayer candles after the candles themselves have burnt away. If Parker ever really does come back here he's going to have to enter the house, finally, or else sleep in the leafy dirt, because his tent is not habitable in its present condition, having been turned by Katy into the world's first and only anarchist shrine.

Thomas has a somewhat different interpretation of Parker's flight. He thinks that a basically good punk finally let his own bullshit get the best of him and lost his fucking head. He likes to think that Parker will come to his senses, develop some genuine revolutionary consciousness in place of all this hoodoo. Or that maybe he did, and that that was what set him running—escape from the tyranny of Katy's eager discipleship. He could be out there doing stuff with Earth First! or something else awesome. He could be with the Ruckus Society, getting ready for Seattle in November. But that's probably just Thomas's romantic streak talking, because it's where *he* wants to be—putting his skills, himself, his body, to some *use* in this world, instead of hiding out here in this sleepy college town, praying for rain. Even an atheist Jew like him knows that old spiritual about how it's gonna be the fire next time. Thomas wants to be kindling, or better yet, a STRIKE ANYWHERE match.

Realistically, Parker probably played the long odds once too often and is in jail somewhere for shoplifting and/or vagrancy. Or if he's still free he's probably the same as ever, only worse—out in the Southwest maybe, ranting at the crazy-making moon. One way or the other, Thomas doesn't think they'll ever see him again. Though God knows he's been wrong before.

For example, he assumed that after Parker left, Katy and Liz would start to get over all his horseshit. How could they not, right? The guy sold them out like a million different ways. Thomas stopped arguing with Katy about Parker because it seemed QED to him that she'd let the thing die, find something else to project all her passion onto—hell, he thought they'd be a Food Not Bombs house by now. It astounds and disgusts him that instead Katy has continued Parker's work and developed this weird little following within the community of Gainesville anarcho-punk: a sub-sub-subculture. And never mind that its very existence puts to question the ethos it ostensibly champions. Nobody hated crowds and groups like Parker. He could barely stand to have *friends*. Well, perhaps twisting Parker's call to radical solitude into the pretext for punk rock love-ins is Katy's true and lasting revenge on her AWOL master, though Thomas does wonder if the perversion is conscious. Anyway, don't most disciples wind up turning their masters' work inside out? So isn't this really like the most typical, banal thing imaginable? The pattern is the breaking of the pattern—or whatever the fuck it was Parker used to say. Who has time for this Deleuze and Guattari meet Kierkegaard shit?

They gather at Fishgut on Sunday nights, biweekly, to get wasted and talk about their socio-spiritual development. They trade shoplifting tips and talk about energy projection and polyamory, or worse yet, read their poems to each other. Sloppy orgies break out on the living room couches, or the far dark corner of the porch. Someone invariably remembers there's paint under the sink and then more New Age neo-Pagan pseudo-Gnostic (who can tell the difference at this point?) drivel sprouts up on the walls like bright stupid flowers. Thomas could, maybe *should* make a point of being elsewhere when they come over, but then it's like who the fuck are they to run him out of his own house? Plus sometimes someone brings a guitar, or he gets his cock sucked. The main thing is to hide in his room during Katy's homily, and/or, Jesus save us from ourselves, the open mic.

But tonight is different from all other nights, because something has happened that he can't explain. Katy's never been a liar, but if there's one thing he's learned during his accidental fieldwork among the true believers, it's that you can't account for the lies people tell to themselves and then believe. If it had been Liz, he'd have said she made it up to please Katy, because that's the kind of bug-eyed follower, pushy bottom that Liz is. Hell, even if it had been David—

his old friend found then lost again so quickly this whirlwind week—he would have seen right through it. Wayward soul punch-drunk on double helpings of pussy, more than willing to play the mark in this dyke conspiracy, totally unconcerned with whatever the big picture is actually a picture of.

But Anchor wouldn't let Katy put her up to something like this. She just wouldn't. And even if she had—which she didn't, because she wouldn't—Thomas would know it, because Anchor has tried to lie to him before (about not coming from money, or where she was last night) and he can always tell. He doesn't call her out, because they're not into that kind of reproach and contest. Hell, they're not even exclusive—just in love. And he gets why she wouldn't want to share certain things. Liz is genuine working-class trash, as are Owl and Selah. (Katy and Parker he's not sure about—their pasts are unknown to him, their respective personas cut from whole cloth. It would surprise him zero to learn that one of them was a trailer park brat and the other a Trustafarian; what he can't decide is which one might be which.) But Thomas, David, Anchor—their parents don't punch time clocks. They came to Gainesville through the VIP door, i.e., the college, and it's a very hard thing to be fresh from that, or still partway in it, like Anchor is, and have to figure out how to look these truly fucked people in the eye and call yourself kin with them—brother, sister, ally—and not secretly believe you're just a lifestyle tourist, an interloper, a piece of duplicitous shit like the girl in that rad Tilt song "Molly Coddled," or that Pulp song "Common People," the latter of course being too techno-ish to ever cop to having listened to, much less enjoyed, but still. Anyway, what's the solution? All you can do is live in contradiction—a state of faith, basically—until the pressure sends you screaming back to campus or else the lie becomes true. As for Thomas it proudly has.

As for Anchor, he's sure, it will.

So he knows that what Anchor says happened is what she really does think happened, though he hasn't had a chance to actually talk to her, only listened in a little on them fawning over their dug-up book, then cranked his music up again to drown them out. Apparently Parker kept a diary, or something. Wonders truly do never cease. In any case, what *actually* happened may be—has, in fact, *got* to be—something else again from what they all seem to be claiming to each other (visions! prophecy!) but knowing that she isn't lying is a start. He isn't sure what kind of subconscious autosuggestive *X-Files* shit might be going on here, but he knows he's never going to figure anything out sulking off by himself. Which is why he's in the bathroom now, checking beneath the mostly dried pink paper towel to see what kind of condition his knuckles are in. The bleeding has stopped. That's good. He tosses the towel in the trash, then goes back to his bedroom to get dressed for the evening service.

They come trickling through the wide back gate, not two by two like you'd imagine, but in ones and threes, clusters that seem somehow isolate, tripartite bodies straggling through the steam-close Floridian dark. They gather about the fire pit, flasks unsheathed from pockets, three or four rolling smokes from a communal pouch of shag. One kid wants to use the bathroom, and so breaks off, lets himself in through the kitchen door—nobody knocks here, nothing's locked, everything is permitted—and Thomas takes a step aside, his back pressed against the fridge, out of the path of the kid's ingress.

"Hi," Thomas says.

"Oh hey," says the kid. "I'm Aaron. Is it your first time here, too?"

"Yeah," Thomas says. "You could say that."

"Cool, man. Very cool. I've heard it's like amazing and also like—kind of pretty fucked-up."

"Weirder the better, right?"

"Fuckin' A," Aaron says, and then is onward again to the bathroom, except there's already a line for the bathroom three people deep, so they're backed up to the edge of the kitchen, so actually Aaron doesn't go anywhere at all. He's stuck right where he is. To keep things from getting awkward, and also because it was the original goal anyway, Thomas walks out through the still-open door.

Katy isn't out here. She always stays secluded in her room for the hour or so before she goes on. Preparing, she says, emotionally and spiritually—meditating or jerking off or whatever it is she does. Thomas thinks the whole thing stinks of theater, though on this day of all days it makes a kind of sense. Probably she's holed up with the precious Book of Parker, poring over its rambling pages, fretting how there's hardly enough time to cobble together anything like a coherent homily—not that her regular homilies are anything close to coherent, in the traditional sense of that word. Though in fairness, that's an assumption; he's never bothered to sit through one since they've moved here. Perhaps she's gotten better—it's possible—though the next thing that occurs to him is: *better at what?*

He walks through the crowd of kids, counting heads and, at the same time, familiar faces. He figures about fifteen attendees, including the handful inside. But that's *not* counting Owl and Selah, who are here because they know there'll be food after and are too polite to hide out in their van until it's served. Besides which, as hippies, they have a basically limitless capacity for suffering bullshit. In fact, except for the blessed absence of heroin, they're kind of collectively Drake the junkie all over again.

Thomas is also not counting himself, or any of the other housemates. So the total number of people present is higher—probably twenty or twenty-two.

Of the nonresidents assembled, figure about three quarters of them are friends, or at least faces he knows from the scene. People he's done sound for, served food, or had to for whatever reason forcibly eject from some show. These are the ones he walks past, wordless, nodding curtly back at the ones who acknowledge him, which are several. And why not? In a tight scene like theirs in a small town like this, he's basically a celebrity, only half a rung down from the local gods who are actually *in* bands.

Thomas is headed toward the tent where, apart from the group, stand Anchor and Liz. The girls are not talking, or even looking at one another. Each has her attention focused on an object—Liz on the shade-drawn window of her and Katy's and David's bedroom; Anchor on the dull dumb tent, restored immediately after the excavation project to its exact original plot. The general congregation might as well not even be here. Ah, elders and acolytes, you can see it already, how they're just like every other sicko cult in history. At least that's how it looks to Thomas, but then again, it's early yet. Barely past nine o'clock.

The girls register his presence more or less at the same time. Anchor breaks out this grin that lights her whole face up like a jack-o'-lantern. Liz, however, has the opposite reaction; there are storms out on the waters in her flashing eyes, and she steps forward, boldly putting her body between the tent and Thomas, as if she expects him to attack it—as if she thinks she can stop him if he does.

"Listen," he says, but the words aren't coming. "Chr— fuck. I don't know, okay? I'm here."

Anchor brushes past Liz, throws her arms around his neck and herself into his arms. Hot-blooded thin girl, wild with both vicious independence and seething need, pooled sweat ever present at the nape of her neck, beneath the tied-back thicket of her high-density dreads, the secret nest where he has his face buried. He squeezes her tight enough to break her, to make sure that she knows that he knows that she won't.

But of course their little moment isn't happening in some vacuum. Guarded, nervy, edgy Liz is here, watching and processing and just having to cut in.

"Your name means doubt," she tells Thomas in a dead voice. He pulls his face away from his shuddering girlfriend's neck.

"Like, etymologically?" he asks, knowing damn well what she actually means but betting she won't know what he does. It sure is nice to be smarter than people.

But their war or whatever is going to be delayed yet again, because a hush falls over the neglected crowd behind them, and this booming silence can only mean one thing.

They part for her like curtains, the throng, as she approaches. She wears a plain black tee shirt missing its left sleeve, and a dirty-white ankle-length skirt with small floral embellishments at the hem. She's barefoot, and there's something different about how she's walking. It's not tentative, exactly, but it's slow. She moves as if through an atmosphere of high viscosity, overlaid upon or coterminous with the plane of being the rest of them are in, but accessible to Katy alone. Her face is purposefully rid of expression, she's a blank screen, and despite her having napped she looks beleaguered, worn down, as if this thing she's so long hungered for and expected has turned out to be more burden than she can bear.

Is there anything more terrifying than a dream come true? If so, it's almost certainly an answered prayer.

After she passes through their ranks they regather. They bunch up and follow behind her like a wedding train.

These "services" began as a joke. One Thomas personally never thought was funny, but still. It was a pointed heresy, an excuse to party on schedule. The model is the Jewish Sabbath, beginning after instead of at sundown, and set on Sunday/Monday, as both an affront to traditional Christianity and as an affirmation of the anarchist principle of Zerowork. Monday as the official Day of Rest—isn't that hilarious?—to be spent lazy and hungover or else drunk again, while the rest of the zombie world slouches off to another degrading week at the office, the big-box store, the corporate chain restaurant, the capitalist workhouse in all its manifold and secret forms.

The reverence for Parker—not his teachings, but him as a person, this idea of him as a holy man—began as a kind of joke, too. His earnestness, implacability, and penchant for disappearance—Katy respected these things immensely, and yet could not help but laugh at them sometimes. When he was gone in the woods (or on the prairie; whatever it was) Katy had sometimes referred to him as the Hidden Imam of Anarchy. Then he came back all grave, mumbling gnomic "wisdom," then left again so soon and in his absence the myths resurged, only Katy wasn't sure she was kidding anymore. And Liz of course was only too eager to salute whatever flag Katy might fly.

Over the months they've been holding these meetings, the energy has more than merely maintained itself. The revelry has intensified by exponents, and though the congregation's numbers creep rather than surge, its growth is consistent. When exactly, during all of this, did the irony begin to dissipate? Was the shift steady, or was there a tipping point? Thomas doesn't know, because up until today he's made a mostly successful career of ignorance from all this. If Anchor hadn't gotten caught up, he wouldn't even be here now. Ah, but she has been, and so he finds himself beside her, his injured right hand grasping her left one, the two of them stepping back in unison to one side—Liz, alone, steps to the other—so Katy can pass between them and approach the tent.

Katy carries a prayer candle, yet another, from the cache in her closet. This one, Thomas notes, honors St. Sebastian, who was shot full of arrows and yet lived, so they had to kill him twice. The candle is new, virgin wick still white and waxed over. Katy glances at Liz, who steps forward and silently proffers a red Bic. Katy kisses her girlfriend's hand, then nods at her. Liz steps back to her place. The crowd is gathered close about them in a half-moon. Thomas for the first time notices David among the congregants, wearing a pair of tattered denim shorts and a red tank top. In this getup, and newly bearded, David could be a total stranger. In fact, Thomas thinks, he basically is.

Now Katy turns to Anchor, who squeezes Thomas's hand once (he winces but says nothing; she doesn't know about him punching the wall) then releases it and steps forward. The women get close together and lock eyes.

If this isn't choreographed then what the fuck?

They're all just on some level.

Time feels as if it's stopped.

When she's ready, Katy hands the lighter to Anchor and holds the candle up. Anchor brings the Bic to flame on the first try but it winks out in her trembling hand. She does it again and this time they get the candle lit. Katy nods and Anchor steps back next to Thomas but does not retake his hand. Katy drops to her knees—slowly so as not to snuff the candle—and places the glass in its appointed spot, the small round hole in the earth before the tent. She reaches out and with her left hand grabs the metal tag on the zipper. She zips the tent flap fully open with one smooth movement, a perfect arc.

The candle can hardly be expected to light the scene. Night floods from the tent mouth, the pinky-joint flicker in the dirt like a paper boat set adrift on a lake. But Thomas is close enough to see into the gloom without straining. He sees the notebook standing upright, face out, given pride of place amid the forest of hollow glass, dead-eyed saints and saviors by the dozen, at maximum density across the fabric floor of the low and narrow space. On the tent's back wall in telltale black Sharpie, slightly blurred because the ink's bled into the khaki fabric, is the arrow-shot heart inscribed with the anarchist A. Parker's mark.

Was it always on the wall like that, or is this artwork new?

After unzipping the tent, and bowing low over the candle, close enough to feel its rising wisp of heat, Katy stands up and moves to the side so everyone else can see, too. The crowd knits closer together and edges forward. There's grumbling as people jockey for position or complain that they can't see. Katy lets the moment spool itself out until everyone is settled. She reaches into the tent. Her fingers alight on the top edge of the notebook and the touch jostles the tight-packed glass, producing a short volley of unmusical clinks. Chastened by this sound, as if it were a warning, she slows herself down, now working with enormous care to remove the notebook from the tent. At a certain point Thomas realizes he's holding his breath.

It's so easy to get caught up in the moment, and let this shit infect you! Can you imagine being raised like this? Poor Parker must have never had a chance.

When the book is finally extracted, Katy takes it to her chest and holds it tight like a teddy bear, then turns for the first time this evening to face her congregation. She opens the notebook without looking at it—still gazing out at them—so either the selection is random or else she marked the page earlier. Absolute faith or absolute artifice—huckster, angel, medicine show, chosen one, confidence scheme—there's just no way to know, or even guess. Her pupils are enormous, big dark buttons like stuffed-animal eyes as she strains to see in the larger darkness of night, the candle at her back now, she shifts her gaze down to the book in her hands and begins to read aloud.

When she's finished reading she snaps the journal closed and flips it face out, lifts it with both hands like a trophy up above her head, amid scattered whistles and claps. People are glancing around, curious to see who looks wholehearted and who is hedging, not yet ready themselves to commit. But the inertia of crowds is at work here, or else the Holy Spirit is, and before they know it they can feel the feather-light sting of their own palms beating together.

Is that *my* voice I feel rising up inside me like a water jet, spouting forth *Hallelujah?* Shouting *Glory in the Name?* Is that *me* with my arms around these brother and sister strangers, my me-ness dissolving into us-ness, oceanic, and everyone so glad to be free of everything, not least of all ourselves, as we join arm in arm in arm together, every soul-sick idea about limit swept away?

It's a lot of them, all right, but not Thomas. And not Owl and Selah, either. He sees them at the far end of the yard, their backs to the scene, slipping away around the side of the house. Too much even for them, apparently, which truly says something—says everything, really.

So what happens now?

The ululation tapers and is soon enough replaced with genial chatter as people become themselves again. Hey, good to see you. Yeah, you too. How's it going? Katy heads inside with the notebook. It'd be nice to think of it out there in the tent, enshrined and accessible, but the humidity would destroy it in a week. Liz asks if anyone can help her move a few cases of beer, and someone says sure, yeah, that'd be cool.

They have a guy—congregant? parishioner? comrade? lover? friend? whatever; they have a guy—who works at the Publix grocery store on Thirty-fourth Street. He tips them off when good shit is being tossed out. The Publix dumpster fills up almost nightly with more technically-expired-but-totally-consumable food and drink than they could ever possibly make use of. Some nights there's enough to fill Owl's bus twice over, though usually they ride out there on their bikes, fill their backpacks and their baskets, leave the rest behind for the next enterprising troupe of young bums. But nights when they hold services are different—reveries, blowouts—and so they always start stocking up a few days in advance.

In addition to the several cases of beer, they also have the following: eight loaves of bread (white, whole wheat, seven-grain, raisin; take your pick), a crate of oranges, five boxes of Frosted Flakes, four grab-n-go rotisserie chickens in microwave-safe warming bags, a few blocks of extra sharp cheddar, six jars of chunky salsa (mild and hot, but no medium), a cardboard box entirely full of heads of lettuce, several bunches of bananas too mushy to eat but perfect for making smoothies with (though they have no blender), some half-thawed frozen steaks they're not entirely sure about (but are hesitant to chuck, since they're expensive as hell, besides which something died to make them), three family-size bags of baked tortilla chips (perfect complement to the salsa—praise be to the dumpster God), and two buttercream-frosted birthday cakes. All they had to steal was the bag of paper plates.

Katy's in her favorite spot in the living room, the armchair, showing the notebook to some of the more zealous among her flock, but Thomas notices that there are only a few of these. Everyone else has had their fix and fill; they're ready to get on with their night. Not even Liz is over there (though David is); she's in the kitchen sipping a bottle of expired High Life and watching as a buzz-cut-sporting girl Thomas thinks is named Cindy slices up one of the cakes with a fine shining knife from David's salvaged block.

Cindy—or whatever her name is—hands Liz a yellow paper plate with a fat slice of cake on it. The cake is dark chocolate and the icing is bright white, a snowdrift in full sun, save for a single red rose of frosting. "That looks good," Thomas says. "Can I have one?"

"Sure, man," maybe-Cindy says. "Anyone good coming up at Clasen's?"

"This Bike Is a Pipe Bomb," Thomas says. "And hopefully the Dust Biters, but I'm not sure when."

"Well, cool. You should let me know. Maybe we could meet up there or something."

"Yeah, maybe, sure."

Thomas's plate is blue. He passes through the kitchen, grabs three beers from the case in the fridge—all with his left hand, the bottlenecks between his fingers—and takes his spoils back to his room, hip-bumping the cracked door wide, then nudging it closed behind himself with a foot. He puts everything down except for one beer, twists the cap off, and lets the little puckered button fall. He turns his stereo on, punches PLAY on the tape deck, and sort of half sits half drops to his own floor while the speakers hiss. He leans his back against his bed, reaches up behind his head and feels around for the plate. Maybe-Cindy didn't give him a fork. Ah fuck it. Poison Idea is singing "Death Wish Kids" at stun-gun volume and Thomas is eating liberated cake with his bare hands.

But the Poison Idea album's only like twenty-five minutes long, and he started it in the middle, so it's over way too soon. He thinks about rewinding the tape and starting from the beginning, but maybe better to see what comes on next.

"There's a fire in the Western world!"

Oh fuck it's Dead Moon! They're this amazing lo-fi punk trio from—where are they from? Oregon somewhere, but not Portland, which *is* where Poison Idea comes from. Somewhere up there. What a weird album this is, *Strange Pray Tell*. Like it'll be raging one minute, really calling the thunder down, but then there'll be a weepie like "Can't Do That," which but for want of a synthesizer and a cheesy big drum would fit comfortably on any Elvis Costello record between, say, *Armed Forces* and now. And then what do they follow *that* up with? "13 Going on 21," with the woman—the bass player— singing in this growl like Courtney Love without the sinus problems. Actually, the whole record sounds sort of like a bootlegged Nirvana demo. Didn't this come out around the same time as *Nevermind*? Close, anyway. Must have been. The Great Northwest. Jesus Christ. What he wouldn't give to have been able to be there then, know those guys, witness everything firsthand, be part of it. He was a kid, of course, still in high school when Kurt made his big decision. After

Kurt died the whole scene imploded. The replicas swept in—vulturous scum like that band Bush, and then all that hideous pop-punk that still dominates today. NOFX and all that shit. Ugh. The whole Fat Wreck Chords catalog should just die already—except for Propagandhi of course. Because those guys come from a metal background, and their politics are A fucking plus.

This album's really not that punk at all, actually. At least not soundwise. Closer to country music and, like, the Replacements or something. But that's the whole thing about punk, isn't it? What bands like Blink-182 can't understand—punk isn't a sound, it's an idea. It's a posture, if there's a way in which saying that can be a not-pejorative thing to say. Or, if there isn't, then put it another way: it's a philosophy, not a formula.

Fuck, but he sounds like Parker, doesn't he? This is fortune cookie logic. Enough, enough. Think about something *useful*, man. You don't want to be like them.

So he thinks about Seattle, and how the New World Order is coming. They'll gather at the end of November, to eat caviar and suck each other off. Unpayable bank loans for the third world; economic slavery as the new face of imperialism. Indian villages drowned by dam projects. Whole forests wiped out so Americans can wipe their asses with two-ply. Countless species vanishing, and the seas rising, and this ragged hole in the atmosphere widening, and skin cancer rates skyrocketing, and a million other things besides. But these guys and their Armani suits. Their silk ties. Filet mignon. Death merchants. Capitalists. Their private cars and mobile phones.

Thomas has never been to Seattle. Hasn't been much of anywhere, in fact, which always bothers him when he thinks about it—and then the being-bothered is what bothers him because it's such a problem of privilege. Some people live under power lines, or grow up in the middle of some refugee camp, or sweat their childhood out in some factory or mine. Thomas's biggest bitch in life is that the family only ever took vacations to see his aunt on Long Island, plus of course the occasional cruise. What's next? Complaining that they never sent him to Europe? Actually, his mom thought studying abroad was this totally great idea for his junior year, and had been more than willing to pay for it, but then he dropped out instead. Okay, slow down. Nobody can control where they come from. It's not your fault your father played markets. And again, it's not like he's a Rockefeller. His parents both still work. The nest is pretty much feathered, but it's hardly gilt. And it's not like he takes their money anyway. Not like they offer. "When you're ready to behave like an adult," they said, "we can discuss how to fund your going back to school. Until then, there's really nothing to talk about." Too true. And so he hasn't talked to them in *how* long?

Ah, but he's really getting into it tonight, isn't he? Time to crack another beer.

Seattle. City of wind and grunge, heroin and hi-tech and, uh—what else? Starbucks. Aren't they from there? And Nike, maybe. Yeesh. Still. The WTO protest is going to be a *big* deal. He's sure of it. Seattle's going to be a game-changer. The movement is going to make itself known, take the overlords by surprise for once, and declare with one resonant voice that another world is possible, and we demand it be delivered to us now. After that—well, who knows? If they can win big in Seattle then anything might follow. This could be the beginning of the new New Left. Maybe they'll be able to light a little fire under that fake-ass progressive Al Gore. If he wants to run for president next year he's going to have to distance himself from Blow-Me Bill's neoliberal scam job. That hayseed motherfuck. Air strikes in Africa, more pot smokers arrested than under Nixon, telecom de-regulation, the extraordinary unchecked violence of "free trade," the promise of health care betrayed, plus whatever *actually* happened to that Vince Foster guy. When this is what the liberals look like, who needs conservatives? This whole bullshit line about the "global village." Stinks about as rotten as "two-party system." They just want to solidify their position. New command and control centers for the capitalist war machine. Time to sound the alarm loud and clear, wake the world up from this fucked fever dream, and that's what it's going to be all about in Seattle.

"Man with no eyes appears," sings Dead Moon. Or, really, moans it. Then something something, "room 213." He's never been able to figure this song out. The only thing he knows for sure about it is it's a minute and a half too long. Maybe there's a reason these guys never sold out when grunge broke big. Like, maybe nobody offered.

Thomas downs the last of his beer and picks himself up off the floor. He puts the bottles on his windowsill, looks out across the dark front yard. There's light in the VW, soft and small: more candles, he's almost sure of it. It's like the Middle fucking Ages in this family. He turns from the window, hits the STOP button on the tape deck. When Dead Moon winks out of existence it is instantly replaced not with silence but with the noise from the living room. There's a full-blown party going on out there. There's a fire in the Western world.

He's in the bedroom doorway now, appraising the scene. He'd like to lock his door, but you can only do that from the inside. Not like anyone's going to steal anything—not like he has anything worth stealing, except the stereo, which is too bulky to move without someone noticing. His real concern is that nobody ends up screwing on his bed. Nobody but him, that is. So he shuts the door firmly, as in, *people take heed.* Not that anyone's paying attention to him, but he at least knows what he meant.

Now he's back in the kitchen, shouldering his way through clusters of kids in conversation ("yeah the problem with Chomsky," "and my sister was all like," "you missed that show how could you miss that fucking show it was the best show I ever saw I can't believe") on his way to the beer. He's both astonished and impressed to see how low supplies are running. This crowd's got appetite, that's for sure. If there was only some way to harness that energy for anything remotely useful. He grabs two of the last beers, jams one uncomfortably into his pocket and cracks the other, takes a big swig, then surveys the traffic jam of bodies that fill all the floor space, halls and doorways, slouched on couches, leaning against walls. Where did all these other people come from? He turns the other way, out the kitchen door again, past a loose clutch of chattering smokers in their dingy convivial cloud.

He sees a circle of poets over by the tent, gathered close about the candle's sunken light. Anchor's with them. This is her favorite part of the service, to sit and listen and clap for her friends. She never brings anything of her own to share, has never tried to write a poem, she says, but Thomas is pretty sure she'd like to. Maybe she's working up the guts. What he would like is to grab her attention—whisk her away to his room, where they can talk and screw, but it would be wrong to drag her from this moment. Because she really *would* come, if he asked her to. In fact, he should go away before she notices him standing there, because if she sees him it won't be about her anymore, it'll be about what he hears, his opinions and approval: him him him. It makes him wary and nervous, the command he has over her. He'd break her of it if he only knew how.

In the unlit side yard, some guy who apparently ran out of patience with the bathroom line is pissing on the side of the house. He's got both palms flat against the wall like a suspect, his dick swinging free. A short ways beyond him two girls, who obviously had this spot long before pisser arrived, are rolling around on the ground and kissing, leaves clung up all over their tee shirts. Thomas steps literally over them as he passes into the front yard.

The slide door of the VW is closed, but the small light within is still shining, and they're not making fuck noises or anything, so Thomas knocks.

"Oh, hey man," says Owl, popping up from the floor of the van, his face filling the window: a pair of Coke-bottle glasses beneath a floppy rainbow Rasta hat. He'd be a perfect cartoon if not for the beard stubble. And the worry lines. How old is Owl, anyway? Closer to Rooster's age than Anchor's. Yikes.

Owl slides the bus door open and Thomas climbs in. There's music coming from a small beat-up boom box that's plugged into the extension cord that snakes out the bus's front window, an umbilicus connecting it to the house. The music is hippie shit—aimless, all high-end, and on these speakers might as well be coming over a tin-can tree house phone. But hey, to each their own. Right? Selah's stretched out on the back bench. The guys both sit cross-legged on the floor, where the middle bench should be but isn't. This is where they sleep, on a foam pad that's presently rolled up and stuffed under Selah's seat. For once, she's not making a necklace, but her hands are still busy at work. She's rolling a fat jay; exactly what Thomas had hoped. "Can I offer you something?" he asks. "A few bucks."

"Nah man, pleasure's ours. This is your juice flowing through our troubadour." He pats the boom box affectionately on its lid, which sets the CD skipping. "Ah *man*." He pops the lid open, pulls the still-spinning disc from the tray, starts to fiddle with something inside. Clearly not the first time Owl's had to do triage on the boom box. By the time the jay's lit the air is once more filled with the sound of breezy, shapeless tin. Now Thomas is feeling fine. Relaxed, a little silly—totally mute. Pot always makes him feel like he's got his head stuck in a cotton ball. A not unwelcome sensation, though sometimes it makes him nervous because he hates to feel like he can't express himself, can't say what's on his mind or pick a fight. But now, here, with these two well-beloved weirdos, in the shabby and substantial comfort of their hot dark van, it is a welcome relief from the polymorphous chaos of the party. He is glad to be confined within himself in silence, no longer cross-legged but now slouching against the van's inner wall.

Selah offers him a small round orange-and-brown throw pillow. He takes it without a word, lets his slouch slide farther into full-on lying down, fixes the pillow behind his aching, swimming head.

Thomas has his eyes closed but is not sleeping. He's listening to the wonderful strange cadence of Owl, who is babbling to his lover about their future.

"Selah, baby. Baby, it's just like that song says. That song says it and it's so. 'Open up your eyes little darling. Been here for 'bout too long.' How long can we keep living in this van? We need to find ourselves a—a place in life, man. We need like a—room. You know? I know you know. But listen. It isn't going to happen here. That's sure. I mean there's just not enough here to make anything off of. There's not enough coming through. What we need is a plan. We need a plan and we'll be golden. We'll think of the perfect plan.

"Can we put that song on, actually? I sure wouldn't mind hearing that song again. You know it's my favorite song there is. After I hear that song I just won't care about anything, but hearing it will help me think. I'll think of our new plan while I listen to it. It's on, um, second disc of *Shining Star* I think. I don't think we even have another recording of that one, actually. It wasn't one of the ones he ever played very much. I don't think I ever even saw him play it, and I went to forty-eight shows.

"Selah, baby, how about Asheville? We could make it in Asheville. I think so. There's plenty of music, and the people are right. I know someone in Asheville. I think he'd let us stay. We could sell the van and save the money. We could figure something out. I feel it, man, I mean I really do. It's like this twinkling light in my mind that knows what the truth is. Now if I could just remember that motherfucker's name. I mean if I could just sort of get my head on straight for a second, put on my, you know, thinking cap, and remember the name of the guy who. Hang on. Okay.

"Okay.

"Okay, it's on the tip of my tongue.

"Okay okay okay okay. Come on now. Come on now, old brain, time to be a genius.

"Fuck.

"Okay let me just not think about it a minute and then it'll come. Too much pressure, you know? Too much pressure which never did anybody any good. God I love this song. I mean I could just listen to it again, and then the whole rest of this album. All Jerry's good Jerry to me, man. But I know you don't really like the nineties stuff. How you say his voice just sounds so old that it makes you sad. I mean I respect the way you feel about that. I can see how a person would feel that way. I mean, actually, in a certain sense, like in the objective sense of whatever, I mean I even feel the same as you, I guess. I mean you put the music on and it's not like we're hearing different music. I hear what's coming out of the speakers, same as anyone. It's just, you know, it's not objective when it comes to him. Music is my religion, baby, and I know you know that, and I know it's yours, too. And that we're the same—denomination, isn't that right? Selah, baby, you know how it is. It's us in this thing together and we've got every good thing coming.

"Hah! I knew I'd get it. I got it. Here it is. Ted, Ted from Asheville. Ted's a real buddy. We go way back. He's true blue. He's gonna be waiting for us when we get there. He's gonna hear my brain waves and know we're coming. He always said if I was ever passing through to stop off and see him. He always said if I ever needed anything at all. Well we're gonna have us a time at old Ted's, Selah baby. Ted is the name that means every little thing will be all right."

Thomas sits up and the world's swirling. He puts a hand out as if to steady himself on a badly shaking train, though of course nothing is in motion. Just him, his head. "Okay, fuck," he says. "Hey listen, thanks so much for the smoke. You guys really saved me."

"Anytime, man," says Owl. Selah says nothing. Now that he can focus his eyes again, Thomas sees that she's rolled over on the bench, asleep. Has Owl been soliloquizing this whole time to nobody? Christ, but they really are made for each other, this poor pair. It's like epically tragic and beautiful, in a kind of white-trash way, how they're always leaving but never actually going, always still just right here. They'll grow old in this van, Thomas thinks, if they don't accidentally drive it off a bridge.

The party peaked, apparently, while he was hanging out with the hippies. Mission accomplished. There are some couch-crashers, plus the requisite last nighthawks out back by the bug light, but basically things have died down. Except in the back bedroom. He can hear punk music of indeterminate vintage and middling quality coming from in there, and below that, the awkward moans and grunts of, say, a half dozen wasted people attempting some miscarriage of human geometry. Thomas stands in the hallway before the door, listening. He of course, like them, believes that marriage is a form of oppression, and that monogamy itself is a patriarchal conspiracy to outfit a politics of domination with the pretense, the mask, of moral virtue—but he's never been able to get into the whole group thing. It seems dangerous, for one, but that's not even the issue. Really it just weirds him out.

The door opens and out stumbles cake girl. She's wearing a different tee shirt than earlier, with no bra beneath it and nothing at all on her bottom half. From her shaved sex dangles a small white string. A sheen coats her pale skin. "I'm just—the bathroom," she says to Thomas as she lurches by. As if he'd asked. Thomas says nothing to her, only looks, gawking, into the orgy room, where it's a thousand degrees even with the window open, and the pit-crotch stink is stunning, and shapes grind in and out of panting shadow. Someone is splayed out on the lower bunk of the nearer bunk bed. Katy is sitting on his face and making out with Liz, who's kind of haunch-crouching over the body. There's a hand in her, but it's unclear whose. Splayed guy's cock is in the mouth of the kid Thomas met earlier (what was his name?) who said he'd heard things were amazing here, but also kind of pretty fucked-up.

If you will it, it is no dream, kid.

Could that supine body they're all working on belong to his old friend David? Prude, private David, the bane of whose middle school years was those five naked seconds while changing in the locker room before and after PE class? David whom he's barely caught sight of all night? Could that be him on this filthy mattress, neck-deep in Katy's nethers even as his own spit-shined cock now fills some random punk's relentless mouth?

The body on the bed begins to spasm, powerful ripples that seem to originate at the belly button and work their way outward: up and down the body at once. The boy on the floor adjusts himself to allow clearance for the splayed body's legs, which now flail on either side of him, as he leans in closer, deeper, and swallows and swallows and still doesn't get it all.

Is this David? Thomas feels like he has to know.

"Hey!" shouts an unfamiliar male voice from the top bunk. "In or out, dude."

"Yeah, no audience, thanks," seconds an equally alien female voice. "Shut the door."

Jolted from his—ahem—reverie, he does what they ask him: shuts the door on the first roar of what sounds like Katy's orgasm, coming close on the heels of the guy's—David's, if it is him, and really, if so then so what? He turns away from the back bedroom to the door of his own room. This doesn't actually require walking anywhere. The two rooms share a wall. And why is *his* door cracked open? Swear to God, if there's anyone in there. If it's that fucking cake girl—

But it's only Anchor, asleep in his bed, curled up, the sheets twisted and kicked off in the heat, the pale freckled curve of her back in the moonlight just about the sweetest thing he's ever seen. She's all angles, elbows and boy hips, every notch in her spine visible. She doesn't go in for that other-room shit, either. It weirds her out, too. She's said so.

My God, this day! This girl—*his* girl, if that's not too fucked-up to say, just once, when nobody's around and he's not even saying it aloud. His sweet girl. What has she gone and gotten herself tangled up with? They still haven't had a chance to talk at all. In the morning, in the morning. He'll tell her about what he's decided—Seattle—and they can figure out what makes sense to do. He'll tell her things like what he heard Owl telling Selah, only it won't be bullshit when he says it, because they're not a couple of addle-brained hippies. And because they're not old. Anchor won't be in school this fall. She'll be on a train somewhere, or hitching, or hiding out from the Oklahoma rain in an abandoned barn like a desert island in the middle of the golden wheat-sea. And wherever it is, she'll be with him and he'll be with her. And who knows? Maybe they'll want to try monogamy; see where it gets them. It's not like committing to a person means you automatically become some sellout. People have the right to do whatever works for them. The anarchist as monarch of the freed self, right? That's a Parkerism. Even a broken clock is right twice a day.

He can't wait to start making their plans. In fact, he's half tempted to wake her up right now—but no. That's no good. She's had a hard enough day, beguiled or whatever by Katy, tricked into thinking she's part of some divine fucking mystery. Let her sleep it off. It'll all make sense in the morning.

But instead of climbing into the bed, he steps back into the hall. He heads for the living room, where it's dark. He pads past the sleepers wheezing in their alcoholic oblivion, over to the bookshelf where Katy keeps Parker's precious library: all the books he collected when they lived at the Coop and left behind when the squat got broken up. Katy saved them. A whole suitcase full of Christian gobbledygook and anarchist theory—as if any book could teach a person how to live.

Thomas finds the notebook just where he thought he would: face out, propped up by earmarked-to-shit copies of *Future Primitive* and the *Summa Theologica*. That is: Zerzan and Aquinas, dead center of the bookshelf, the fault line where anarchy and Jesus meet.

What did Parker *do* out there in the wild, alone for so long? Did he eat nothing but berries until his waste slid out of him like water, not even worth digging a hole for? Did he eat carrion? Hunt game? Did he sneak into town and raid dumpsters? Surely he was too filthy, stank too bad, to pass unnoticed in any store. Did God give him manna? Did he simply sit in his tent and meditate on the terrible memory of Drake's corpse, while the sun and moon wheeled in and out of the sky unseen above his weather-resistant polymer roof? Was he writing this book the whole time? Did he starve himself mad?

Thomas takes the notebook to the kitchen. He opens it and starts flipping pages. He's looking to see if there's any consistency to Parker's writing style, or if he always used the same kind of pen. Anything telling. But no, the journal's a mess. Some entries are dated, others not. There are all kinds of ink colors—blue, black, a good bit of purple. Some of it is his own writing, some of it is quotes he saw somewhere and copied over. Sometimes there's just a few lines on a whole page, like he was going to come back to it later but never did, like here:

Why should religion be useful in your everyday life? Why should politics be pragmatic, or worse yet, practical? True religion, like true political will, seeks nothing less than the destruction of the everyday, the eradication of the normal and the usual—the call to Stand Apart is, in the end, not a permanent injunction. When your Action doesn't merely take a side or tip a scale, but actually alters or overturns the terms and conditions of the false oppositions that govern the everyday, then and only then is it Right. There *will* come a time for Right Action.

What a fucking joke this whole thing is. What he *should* do is take the notebook outside right now and burn the son of a bitch, nip this thing in the bud.

But Thomas has other, bigger plans. He opens the kitchen's random-shit drawer and fishes out a blue Bic pen. Weird how those are the two main things the company makes— lighters and pens. What's that about, anyway? Okay, Thomas, time to focus. He figures it's not worth it to try to imitate Parker's handwriting. He's better off just trying to do a quick, nonspecific scrawl and hope that it blends. Not like Parker's handwriting is so unique. It's erratic and loping, rather childish, actually.

Thomas laughs under his breath, a hushed and ugly sound. In the notebook he writes:

Desire is a strange attractor. Your longing warps the arc of the world's emergent truth.

He puts the notebook back on the shelf where he found it. He goes to the bathroom, where he finds cake girl passed out in the tub. Turning the light on doesn't seem to disturb her at all, but he's careful to pee on the porcelain so the water doesn't burble and when he's finished he doesn't flush. He shuts the light on his way out. "Huh?" he hears her say to no one in particular, apparently roused by the resurgent dark. Absolutely not his problem. He goes back into his bedroom, closes the door gently behind himself, so quietly it doesn't even click. He locks it. He strips down, conscious of the explosive thumping of his heart in his chest, and beyond that the muffled music from the madhouse next door. The gravity of what he's done is beginning to set in. Okay, come on now. Just a practical joke. It's late, and you've got a lot to do tomorrow. He tries to think happy thoughts, like how after him and Anchor are set up in Seattle, probably after the protests, he'll want to start a band. Anchor doesn't know how to play anything, but he's pretty sure she'd be willing to learn. Or she could always just sing. So much possibility. He takes a few deep breaths, does a couple of neck rolls, then climbs gingerly into the bed and eases up next to his girl. She stirs but doesn't wake as he presses his front against her back and wraps his arms around her, his good hand on her bony hip, and the fingers of that hand splayed out across the warm flat of her belly. For the second time today Anchor is somebody's little spoon.

THE LEAVING KIND

The great enemy of strong faith is not faithlessness, no. It is weak faith.

But what *is* faith? We don't ask this enough—ever, really. What does it mean to have it? To keep it? What are its limits and what—if anything—lies beyond? From Parker they know that faith is rooted in what Chesterton called the scandal, and Kierkegaard the absurd. They prefer the latter because it makes for easier conflation with the injunction to *"be realistic: demand the impossible!"* as Peter Marshall has it in the frontispiece to his *History of Anarchism*—also quoted in Parker—besides which, Chesterton is such a petit bourgeois prig.

Okay, let's try it. The paradox of faith is the wellspring of its bounty. The unbridgeable gap is a blessing; from it is born the promise of flight. If we could prove these things we believe, that is, if we were able to *know* them rather than *believe* them, then our belief would be extraneous, vestigial, our faith pointless. It is not soul competency that makes our hair grow, or pours the eye-brightening whiskey into the river of our thrumming blood. It is not the priesthood of all believers that raises the sun up in the sky of a Friday morning; neither the muezzin nor the minyan that sends it back down at night.

In the situation of contemporaneousness, remarks Kierkegaard, signs and wonders are an exasperatingly impertinent thing. And this, Katy reasons—check that: *believes*—tells them not merely why so few miracles are visited upon the world, but also why some, sometimes, still are.

When the expectation is absence, what could be more impertinent than appearance?

So God has seen fit to grant them a vision, okay. Why not? Their hearts and souls are open, uniquely primed, and truly, what would make less "sense"—more perfectly evidence and manifest God's sublime impertinence, His perfect refusal of perfection, His holy rebel-king spirit—than this? Bunch of drunkpunks in the armpit of Florida, the self-declared children of two traditions that both refuse parentage. Heretics, nobody will have them; nobody will believe in them—yet—but Him. They are His and He is theirs and there for them. The strength of the absurd.

And of course there are problems already. Errors, shortcomings, flaws, limits, gaps. Inconsistencies and contradictions unresolved and perhaps beyond resolution.

Given the opportunity, Flannery O'Connor might have described Parker as a comp lit grad student gone wrong. And Katy, holy shit—where to start? She's this like Ren-fair refugee turned New Age sexaholic gone all too frighteningly right. A lot of the time, he seemed to be barely putting up with her (or any of them) but the fact remains that he did, and Parker was never one to suffer fools—or anything much—gladly. So there must have been *some*thing there, right? Something that made them real to each other—the God in each calling out to the God in the other.

Or whatever. Sometimes Liz thinks the real miracle wasn't when Katy and Anchor dreamed of the book, but that it actually occurred much earlier, when Katy got Parker to come over to the house in the first place. It was the only time she ever tested her will against his and won.

Katy's longing for Parker is so intense that it can seem like a put-on, a weird protracted role-play, some kind of shuck and jive. In our wink-and-nod culture, the era of the post-everything, nobody speaks like this—without irony, without cynicism, in and of universals, absolutes—unless they're working an angle. Right? Maybe. But the fact is that for better, worse, or weirder, Liz knows, Katy's yearning is as honest as it is fierce. Katy means what she says. She believes herself.

Privately, however, Liz thinks that Katy's longing for their prophet is based on the deep *knowledge* (i.e., not faith, but the presumptive fact) that said longing will never be relieved. What Katy worships is not Parker so much as Parker's absence, and she herself fills the space she has carved out for him, the role he perpetually declines to appear and assume. Liz doubts that Katy knows that she "knows" this. The knowledge is so fundamental that it does not register as information; it is completely integrated into Katy's reality, not a fact of life *on* the ground but *of* the ground on which life takes place, an unknown known.

Liz's own faith, given to wavering at the best of times, has been lately pushed to the breaking point, beyond it, in fact, which is to say: it's broken. Their devotion is as a scourge to her. The doubt she so callously accused Thomas of was really her own all along, and now, finally, it has burnt her up from the inside out. She's a soul-scorched shell.

And if Katy in all her glorious intuition and godliness could only see what's right there in front of her face, she would confront Liz, call her betrayer, denounce her once and for all. But Katy doesn't do that, because she has no discerning vision. She is a believer, period; eternal optimist, half blind. She can't see Liz for what Liz is—deceiver; pathetic—which is, finally, the failing that Liz cannot forgive her lover for, or bear another instant. Katy's failure to see the worst in her registers as a failure to see her at all.

So here's Liz loading up a blue duffel till it's full with clothes and books—all her stuff, what little she has. A few caseless CDs; she wraps looseleaf pages over them for protection, double-folds the corners down. Her one pair of sneakers (she's wearing the boots) tied together by their laces and hung from the duffel strap. Now she's struggling to get the zipper shut. A stitch pops but no seam bursts, thankfully. Okay. It's going to hold.

Katy's on the edge of the bed, beet-faced. David's somewhere behind her, fidgeting, unsure of what to do or say—if anything. He wishes he could be invisible, here but not here. He knows that he should just get up and walk out, leave the room. This thing is older than him; he is a small, late epoch in their long, rich history. He should give them their moment.

Should, but can't. Who, granted witness, could possibly turn his back on the end of history?

Liz keeps herself strong by going over a mental list of every single bit of shit she's ever put up with for Katy's sake: every false assurance given or accepted, every smile faked and male partner welcomed into bed, all in the service of what? A larger and—she thought—transcendent truth: her love for Katy, their love for each other. Is that love really gone now, sacrificed on the altar of Parker? Or has it merely warped into its inverse—this aching rage she feels?

Thomas had the right idea all along. Liz should have left when he did, a month ago, as soon as the book was unearthed. Liz sees now how it was Thomas alone who saw Katy for what she is—pseudo-revolutionary, wannabe Brigham Young. And beneath it all? Just another fucking college dropout dabbling in the sweaty pleasures of the underclass. Barely distinct, in the end, from the men she brings home.

But of course it's not Katy she hates. Not really. Her true fury is—as always, poor girl—aimed inward, directed at herself for having reached her limit. Because why can't she keep up appearances like usual? Why can't she smile wide like before, say the words? Katy wants to pray to a tent—fine. Parker, servant of God—they've been saying *that* for a year now, give or take. So what's the difference whether or not they're kidding? And though nearly as faithless as Thomas, Liz sees the purpose, even finds joy and comfort, in the ritual and romance of religion. If anything, she'd prefer *more* structure and custom, perhaps even—God save us—a Law or two; just little ones. Something to learn by heart and follow. Because for her, sharing Katy's connection to God is not about God, it's about Katy. The body of ritual—practice and language and gesture—is a vessel, a form, to be filled with genuine faith at some future point, maybe, and if not then not, and that's okay, too. Let that secret emptiness abide as a secret, shared between her and the silence.

Even God's absence is His presence. His silence *is* His thunder.

There are times that she's almost believed that. There could, or would have been, more.

But then here's David. He's the problem, because he really *does* believe. His faith is enormous and ever expanding. She's a candle to his furnace—what's that Dylan line? A fire in the sun. He outshines her. Not in Katy's eyes, necessarily, but in Liz's own. His plain and bountiful certainty in the book, the Revelation, Katy's prophecy of Parker's Promise to return to them; it's all a slap in the face to her, a rebuke to her own faithlessness and the thin mask behind which she hides it, plus the constant fear that that mask will fall away, or be stripped from her. She might as well have the number of the beast emblazoned on her forehead, or MYSTERY scrawled scarlet on her thigh.

"Baby," says Katy to Liz, who is leaving, "think a minute. Hang *on.*"

"Don't be angry you weren't chosen for the Dream," David says. "I wasn't either. He has other plans for us." Liz wheels around, eyes wild, gritted teeth flashing in the light.

"Parker was at least an original," she says, and oh boy now here comes the soliloquy. She had promised herself she wouldn't do this, but really who gives a shit anymore? "He was crazy, but at least he was real. And he would have been disgusted by you. By *both* of you. By this whole thing. If he was here he wouldn't stand for it. He'd turn everyone against you, and it would be easy, and then he would turn on them. Because he didn't care about having followers, or even about being right. He just wanted to do whatever he wanted, and be alone. And if he ever does come back, when he sees this he'll just leave again. You're preparing for nothing. You'll never even know he was here."

"*Get out!*" Katy screams at her lover in a shattered-glass growl, a raked-coals roar, and hearing this, something in Liz dislodges. A weight is cut free. This anger of Katy's—it's a marvel; this and this alone is the true miracle; the only one. It's everything she ever wanted and more. To be the focus of her lover's complete attention, the lightning rod, even if it means being absolute Judas. Deep within the devastated landscape of her heart there blossoms a small bright rose of happiness, the bitter satisfaction born when something precious and long-coveted is finally obtained.

The duffel shouldered, sneakers swinging, she leaves the bedroom. They don't go after her. There are people hanging out in the living room, duh, and she knows maybe half of them. They eye her, this figure in the hallway, and she stares at the linoleum, unable to meet their collective curious gaze. They heard the screaming, of course, and so as far as they're concerned she is not leaving of her own volition, but has been exiled, thrown out. She shuffles into the kitchen, meaning to go out the back, and sees David's knife block lying on the counter on its side. Without thinking, she rights it, and while so doing notices a small oval rust-sore, herpetic, low near the handle of the carving blade.

These knives are like triple stainless steel—how is this even possible?

Put another way: is there anything that Fishgut *won't* turn to shit?

She tucks the block up under her arm, like she did on the day she took it from David's apartment. That bad spot notwithstanding (and who knows, maybe it's fixable) the knife set will make a great gift for her mother, and hopefully help smooth things over in terms of her showing up, surprise, to move back home.

They mourn the loss of Liz, yes, but not deeply, because they've got a more practical problem to deal with and nothing should slow them down. They understand that the Giving of the Book unto them has meant their being charged with a sacred Duty. They wish and are determined to disseminate Parker's Teachings, and it seems like they ought to do this by publishing an edition of his Book.

How does one do that, exactly?

Katy and David are lying on their bed; Anchor's kind of half leaning at its foot, at ease but not fully. It's night. The dim light of candle-saints softens all their faces as usual; between that and a joint they shared earlier, everyone's looking positively blessed. But hang on—focus. What was it Anchor just said? Could she repeat that please?

"What I said," Anchor says, "is why don't you make a website?"

"Why would we want one of those?" Katy asks.

"Because," Anchor says, "it would just, like, *be* there. Anyone could get to it, and it'd be free."

"But getting people to sit plugged in to some machine is everything we *don't* want," David says. "It's like the opposite of everything Parker stood for."

"Stands," Katy says.

"What?"

"Stands. You said 'stood.'"

"Oh, right. Sorry."

"Anyway," Katy says, "none of us knows how to even do that. Do you?"

"I could probably figure it out," Anchor says. "I mean, enough people do it, right? And there's programs you can get to help . . ." But she knows, just from looking at their faces, that this ship is never going to sail, has in fact sunk in the harbor already. They're quiet awhile, watching the candles flicker, or whatever. Katy and David reading the tea leaves of Anchor's body language for any kind of sign.

"Oh fuck, I've got it!" Katy says. "We should do it as a zine."

"But how could we fit the whole journal in a zine?" David says.

"Well," Katy says, "what if it didn't have to be, you know, all of it at once? It could be just enough to get people interested—so they wanted to come over and learn more."

Anchor says she can do the layout, easy, once a manuscript is drawn up. They're still wary of the whole computer thing—David especially, it seems—but inasmuch as they don't have to use one themselves, or establish any kind of cybernetic presence, they're willing to let Anchor make their lives easier. They tell her she's really doing them a solid. They're so grateful for her devotion, and this favor, and hell just everything about her, and why doesn't she do more than just the layout; why doesn't she help them edit the book? She shared in the Dream, after all, and is in every sense *one of them*, which they sincerely hope that she knows.

She says that, yes, she knows, and thank you for saying so. And yet she recuses herself from the culling process, says she doesn't believe herself qualified to make those kinds of judgments—it's beyond her and they can't convince her otherwise. They should just let her know as soon as they're ready with a manuscript; she can't wait to get started. And then she says it's getting late, and they invite her to stay, as they always do, in the bed with them, if she'd care to, or else wherever she likes in the house, and she, as always, says thanks but no thank you; in fact hasn't spent a night at Fishgut since Thomas left; insists on returning to her dorm room; they never can understand why.

It's hard to be an editor! They pore over the Book page by page, the two of them, line by line, compare and contrast, trying to figure out—what, exactly? The Book is tangled and scattershot and sprawling. Parker repeats himself, reconsiders, goes back later and makes addenda or scratches things out. It's a personal journal; deep thoughts share page space with scribbled-down phone numbers, train schedules, shoplifting to-do lists, thumbnail sketches of places traveled and people he met there.

Also, the journal is in large part a record of struggle, his own, with theology, theodicy, the flux and waver of belief. David thinks that this is an essential component of the Book, this proof of unending trial—how salvation is lived moment to moment, and grace is a precarious precipice, from which even the righteous may fall at any moment, and fall further yet for the height at which they once stood. Cf. Liz.

But Katy thinks no, this is no way to generate interest, no way to draw people in, get them pumped up and intrigued. *Aroused* is a word she also uses. "When Christians want to put something on a billboard," Katy says, "they don't choose Matthew 27:46, or 1 Corinthians 13:13. Because those things are too complex for a billboard. So what do they go with?"

"John 3:16," David says.

"Right," Katy says. "Why?"

"Because it's easy," David says. "And it's the whole, like, thesis, right there."

Which for David is exactly the problem. He believes that their extraction from the Book should be at least as difficult as the full work itself. He wants this thing, which they have come to refer to as the Good Zine, to be a kind of stumbling block. A challenge. Will you come and try this? Are you worthy of application? He is a maximalist. He wants to include as much material as possible—however many pages a saddle staple can accommodate, and as much text as each page can take. He wants small fonts and no margins. Here, too, Katy has a very different vision. Economy, essence, invitation. These are her watchwords. She is a zealous condenser and extractor, a cutter-away of contexts, generous only with white space—she wants fewer words, large, bold-faced, the *right* and *best* ones (she says) set in the page field like gemstones in a ring. Once people come to us, she assures him, they will have all the time in the world to wrestle with the finer points of Anarchristian—the term is Katy's own—exegesis and praxis. The goal of the Good Zine is limited and simple. "Asses into seats," she says.

"We don't have seats," he says, glumly. "We have a back-yard with a fire pit and a tent."

"Into dirt, then," she says, smirking.

•   •   •

Here is a passage in which Parker considers three interrelated problems: those of subjectivity, doubt, and the physical body.

Can't tell what is belief, or practice, and what is simply my own preference or character traits. I think of how Kierkegaard's whole system is so clearly born of and shaped by his fundamental intolerance for the human. His abhorrence for the established church works as an argument *for* anarchist principles, and for the idea that the highest level of spiritual perfection is the standing-alone before God, but it seems like that vehemence also refracts backwards, shines on the physical body, as if in an attempt to burn it up. The body is the site of all experience in this world. It is through it that we know anything, everything, and certainly God. Why would God wish for us to hate that of which we are shaped, and through which we know the world He made? It doesn't make sense at first. And yet, it begins to almost come together as I find that there is something ineluctably devastating in the idea of a body, the fact of it, that I am it and it is me, entirely, or stranger still the idea that it is not, and that something which is not this body but which "I" still know as "me" shall one day leave it behind. I hate to be this thing that spits and shits and grinds its teeth and yearns for a fuck. Is it possible that the abhorrence of the body *is* the path to finding comfort in becoming spirit, and is this what is meant by "salvation"? But why, then, if I was spirit before and shall be spirit again, should I suffer to be flesh now? There must be a reason that I cannot know, but the not-knowing feels like punishment, and this feeling fuels doubt and pain. Considering these questions drives me into a kind of impotent, childish rage; rage that I should have to wrestle with this question, despair at having to be anything at all. Are we not all crucified on the crosses of our bodies every moment of our breathing lives?

Katy, the sensualist, the inexhaustible, who so far as David can tell has never begrudged, questioned, or regretted either the fullness or the limits of her own physicality, finds this whole meditation off-putting and bleak. Parker must have been having a bad day when he wrote that, she says, because he wasn't always like this—not even *close*. She laughs then in a way that alludes to experience, and David is forced to remember that she—unlike he—has actually known Parker (had she ever *known* Parker?) and he has not. His faith is belated! He's come too late! But what had even Katy's faith looked like before Parker's departure? They had known he was special, but they hadn't had ears yet to hear him or eyes to see. Their faith, in its fully realized form, had sprung up only after his leaving them, and so in a sense they are belated, too. They knew less, it seemed, for having known him, than he does, for having never. *Blessed are they that have not seen, and yet have believed* . . . That's one of Katy's favorite Bible verses. He understands now how it applies to her as well as to him. None of them has yet seen Parker and known him for who he is. When he returns to them, they will all greet him together, as if for the first time: *face to face.*

The body is the site of all experience in this world. It is through it that we know anything, everything, and certainly God. Why would God wish for us to hate that of which we are shaped, and through which we know the world He made?

"Doesn't this get at the heart of it?" says Katy. "Isn't this the crux of what he meant?"

It isn't. At least David doesn't think so. He thinks that she has edited an honest, earnest question into a rhetorical one that now seems to have been posed ironically, which it hadn't been. She wants a book of aphorisms, it seems to him, might yet prefer a broadside. He tells her he is worried she is remaking Parker in her own image, that she is forging an idol in the fire—carving the easy prophecies that she wants out of the difficult gift they've been given.

She turns away from him, furious and hurt, not the den mother now, not the earth spirit or the sex priestess or the good-times punk. She is his lover, whom he has wounded, caught off guard and stung. He feels terrible and sick. He doesn't know what time it is or what day. It's dark out. He's hungry, sober, and ticked off. The bedroom smells like old coffee; he's grinding his teeth. When did they last eat? How long has it been like this, the two of them pitted head to head, huddled over the holy notebook, doing the most important work in the entire world, and how much are they willing to sacrifice to get it done? Are they going to blow apart, get sick of each other like Liz got sick of them?

He goes to hold her and she lets him.

They stay that way awhile, for however long.

Then they set to work again.

They bicker and make up, take ground and give it, read closely and argue over meaning and intent; whole days swallowed up, hands shrieking their way around a clock face.

Finally, they have a manuscript to give to Anchor. It's a strange little chapbook, this Good Zine, uneven, a bizarre commingling of their counterpoised editorial philosophies, alternately wooing and repulsing its reader, here clear as a fortune cookie and there dense as stone, all the words Parker's own as she wanted, save for the section headings, which he insisted upon including, and which they wrote together. The Zine is something that the whole house can take joy and delight in, and which they feel certain is destined to do its appointed Work.

ONLY EVER TO BE GIVEN AWAY FREELY:

THESE FRAGMENTS OF

THE GOSPEL OF ANARCHY

DELIVERED UNTO THE HOUSE OF FISHGUT

BY THE GRACE OF OUR LORD

AND HIS PROPHET PARKER WHO WROTE

THESE LINES AND MANY OTHERS

IN HIS OWN HAND

IN THE SUNSET OF THE MILLENNIUM

AND REVEALED THEM TO US

IN THE SUMMER OF '99

Seven Theses of Anarchristianity

The Pattern is the breaking of the Pattern.

God frees and saves through the twin and inextricable gifts of Anarchy and Grace. We demonstrate our worthiness to receive these gifts by asserting that they are rightly ours.

When Christ spoke of the fulfillment of the Law, he spoke of the obliteration of the Law, because perfection means Stasis, which is Death. As the Christian triumphs over Death so the Anarchist over the Law—there is no difference or distinction between the obstacles, less still among those who triumph over them.

The body is the site of all experience in this world. It is through it that we know anything, everything, and certainly God. Why would God wish for us to hate that of which we are shaped, and through which we know the world He made?

Chaos is older than Creation. The Anarchist walks with God today, even as she hastens the Death of Empire, that all might walk with God tomorrow.

Joy is a better form of prayer than prayer, but prayer is also a better form of joy than joy.

Desire is a strange attractor. Your longing warps the arc of the world's emergent truth.

A Grammar Lesson

What if instead of "no place," *utopia* could be understood to mean "no place in particular"? As in, could be anywhere. As in, *be here now*. Beautiful, absurd things, possible only with God and through God, Who is the ultimate positive value, the universal affirmation that fills the freed space abandoned by the driven-out rulers of the fallen world, the demiurge and all his archons, their dead systems junk-heaped; their long shadows drowned in a lake of everlasting sun. Any place can be no place if you will it. You drive out everything that is not God, and what's left is pure God, here and now. The eternal manifests in the temporal as a rupture, a revolutionary break. It is in this way that our faith makes us crazy in the world.

To be against the archons—the rulers; to define yourself by what you aren't, by what you oppose. At least in the ancient Greek. But the word we use comes also from *anarchia*, medieval Latin, and they used it to describe God's being without a beginning. Something inductive, rather than oppositional. What would Anarchy look like if we simply started calling it Faith?

On Revelation

Why can't we be pure, and alive like fire is, like the Holy
Spirit who baptized in flame and *was—IS—*flame, pure
spirit-fire, or like the living waters in Revelation are? Water
and fire at once, together, inextricable: *A sea as of glass on fire.*
Revelation 15:2. Revelation in whole an anarchist text, *if* read
properly. Downfall of Babylon. Death of Empire.

Fuck Rome.

Good people fought hard at Nicea to see Revelation
included, all that smoke and gold and blood, so that the Book
would forever insist on the truth at the Heart of Paradox,
or that Paradox is the heart itself of truth. It grieves me to
dream of loss, but also there is the relish of anticipation. And
Becoming. Everything is a way station. Let our lives be our
politics and not our politics our lives. Till to love and live be
one. This is what Christ achieved—embodied, *was.*

Is.

Call for Utopia Now!

All talk of practicality and responsibility is just threats and bluffing to keep us from reaching out our hands to find that Heaven lies in reach before us. And you should know that anything you've ever done or considered doing to get there is not crazy, but beautiful, noble, necessary. Revolution is simply the idea that we could enter that secret world and never return; or, better, that we could burn away this one, to reveal the one beneath entirely. You're not the only one trying to find it. We're out here, too, and if We could create a world in which everything that is possible is also desirable, then there would be no possibility of hypocrisy or conflict between desires. Total freedom, in that case, would mean full worldliness, and the pursuit of purity of heart would be indistinguishable from the embrace of every thing and person in the world.

Siste Viator

Thursday, made Toledo, half starved. Slept in a field the first night. Not too buggy. Saw Scorpio above. Feel like I've been fading in and out . . . There are these hidden things . . . Rain dances past the dim streetlights as I wander desolate suburb-blocks, scrounging—rows of houses with their curtains closed—dead silence and stillness, only me moving through the quiet drumming of the drops on the asphalt. I can hear the earth breathing beneath, lawns are such a massacred ideal, and the houses choked and the people inside them cowering in fear of the outside—frightened of Living, frightened of ME. People don't dream here. They are built on assembly lines at cabinet factories. Or their parents were TV commercials for car tires and fraud diets. All diseased with the zombie virus. Anywhere could be here. I can tell this rain won't stop for days.

One God, No Master

Faith is the power by which we leap over the unbridgeable chasm, burst through the wall of the asymptote, realize Heaven on Earth. Grace is us granted that power, the fuel injected into faith's engine, the energy generated from its burning up.

We *will* live without rulers, without rules. We will prostrate ourselves before God almighty, and He will tell us, I love you, you are My equal, and the very Me of Me: *stand tall.*

A True Story

There used to be an anarchist collective in Gainesville that
met at a greasy spoon on Twenty-third Street called Firpo's.
The collective was called the Re-Levelers and there were
four people in it: two couples, boy-girl. So the four anarchists
were sitting around their table, eating the food they had
ordered and which they would pay for, and trying to draft
a manifesto. They were discussing whether to identify the
Re-Levelers as anarcho-communist or anarcho-communal,
and the discussion had gotten fairly heated. The men were
screaming at each other, starting to draw attention to themselves, and ignoring their girlfriends, who were each trying to
get in edgewise some words of their own. Eventually the two
women flipped over a place mat and scribbled out their own
manifesto, declaring their secession from the Re-Levelers
on account of its inherent sexism, and naming themselves
the Anarcho-Feminist Solidarity Brigade. The men were
still arguing with each other, and had not noticed that their
collective had just been weakened by half. The women left
their manifesto on the table for the men to find and rode their
bicycles back to the house where they all lived together, where
they would later tell their bewildered boyfriends, firmly, that
this was no joke; there were indeed now two anarchist collec-
tives in town, and any alliance between the two groups would
have to be negotiated and earned.

The Moral

Politics are boring because they really are irrelevant. No more time should be wasted debating over "issues" that will be irrelevant when we must go to work again the next day. Lives cannot be theorized and theory cannot be lived. Theorists quibble. Thieves scheme. Be a thief—steal your own life back from the state, and the "anarchists," too. All Freedom flows from devotion to God and to the Freedom of God and in God. Devotion to anything except God and God's Freedom is heresy—but rest assured that Hell does not await you upon your death. You will have already lived through Hell, and it will then be too late to escape.

Wrestles with the Angel Kierkegaard

"I supposed that the very beginning of the test of becoming
and being a Christian was for one to be so introverted that it
is as if all the others do not exist for one, so introverted that
one is quite literally alone in the whole world, alone before
God, alone with the Holy Scripture as guide, alone with the
Pattern before one's eyes."

—*Training in Christianity*

K in perpetual rebellion against the established church. Idea
that the idea of Christendom is heresy. Church militant is
salvation; church triumphant is sloth and disgrace. How do
you keep the church militant? How can you plan a permanent
revolt, unless you plan never to win?

K as anarchist, monarch of the freed self—a king in
rebellion against the whole system of kingdoms. He is drawn
to Christ because he is drawn to the absolute and transcendent sovereignty of the individual. The Kierkegaardian self,
even—especially—in the aspect of its infinite suffering, is
God-vast. The dimensions of the human, the individual, are
extended to encompass the universe. God-in-Christ, Christ-
as-God, each another way of describing K's own conception
of what it means to be a complete self. Of course for him this
conclusion is unthinkable, and so he doesn't allow himself to
state it. Amazing to think that the zealous sufferer, who can
look on unblinking and call Abraham a murderer, ultimately

blinks at the prospect of the obvious: naming himself a God, understanding that God's constant act of drawing-toward, His calling of K and of everyone, is not merely a drawing-toward, but a Becoming.

Virtues of Disappearance

Hakim Bey writes of the Temporary Autonomous Zone,
secret utopias that spring up and then disappear with no
trace. In this age of empire—full spectrum dominance, New
World Order, collapse of the Real into Simulation—ephemer-
ality is no longer a mere characteristic, but is become a value.
Affinity groups, squats, Rainbow Gatherings, Burning Man;
whole minor civilizations appearing like mushrooms after
rain, disappearing like sun-burnt mist, untraceable, a vision,
a dream. The holes in the cybernet, the dead spot in the pan-
opticon's eye. We must know our friends when we see them,
like Christians of old Rome wearing the sign of the fish.

On Hypocrisy

But how can we live without being hypocrites when the entire system in which we are ensnared—from which we aspire to disappear completely, but haven't yet—is a thicket of obfuscation, denial, contradiction, and lies? All the terms of our existence and every fact and facet of our culture—America, Western civilization, modernity, whatever—is hypocritical, infinite sin compounded infinitely over an infinite duration. And hypocrisy is *not* the same as Paradox. If Paradox is the generative friction of two truths simultaneously occupying the same point in space, then hypocrisy is the double black hole of two lies. They will say that we are hypocrites because we take from—in many senses, *rely on*—a system whose existence we oppose. This is a fair and accurate critique—Kierkegaard: it is the eleventh hour! confess your sin!—but if it is the worst thing we can be accused of, then our hearts are more pure than they have ever been, and we, knights of faith, are on the proper path, having reduced our participation in the system to a fine point, a knife edge, a leech mouth. If the organism dies, the parasite moves on, or else dies with it. We should be so lucky as to have this problem!

A Different Trip Another Time Another Rain

Got sick in the Badlands so we set up camp early among wild
sage and roaming buffalo. Felt like my guts would rip apart
but the sky was so beautiful it hurt. Felt closer to everything,
like I was all of it and it was me. Terry worried I was sweating too much, dehydration, but I said, If I die in my footsteps, so be it. Got a ride to Fargo the next day and wanted
to get a train but there was a derailment that caused a great
ruckus and stopped all the trains up in the yard so we started
hitching again or tried to but this time it didn't work. You'd
think with all the so-called Christians in this town . . . But
maybe we looked too dirty by this point. Something. A trial.
Ended up sleeping in another field, not wild like before—the
county fairgrounds, muddy, where mosquitoes feasted on our
blood until we finally gave up on sleep ("for the weak," Terry
cries! as we approach the all-night gas station trying to figure
out how we'll make off with the coffee unnoticed, being the
only customers in the place and all—suffice to say that we got
it done) and finally the sun came out and we got a ride from
Fargo all the way to Minneapolis last night, and today made
it the rest of the way to Bloomington. Found some punx
hanging around a quad at the university and they took us in.
Every college town is heaven, each one different but the same,
like hoboing from Gainesville to Gainesville to Gainesville,
a hundred Gainesvilles flung across the country, like stars in
the sky. Fed and warm now; feeling we are truly blessed on
this trip—not that we aren't always, all the time, but it can

be *so* hard to keep in mind. I keep waiting for words that are waiting for me and disappearing into undefinable moments but I know that they are there as love is there, is here, looking at the same stars that are looking down on me and into me, moments perfect without words or they could or should be. I know everything is a way station—me and Terry, only passing through here, only passing through each other's lives—but there's a storm gathering in the gray sky and the rain is also holy—it keeps the leaving kind from disappearing too soon. Holding Terry close, under cover while the storm beats down. That's it.

Olam Ha-Ba

Faith grows in slip-spaces, rough spots, cracks. Give it something to grasp on to, a niche in rock face, a trellis— something to cover or climb. It thrives in the soil of lack, and in its upward-striving breaks the concrete beneath which the buried soul slumbers, dormant, but is yet alive. Only air-tight systems are airless. They self-asphyxiate, as the global capitalists will discover soon enough. The diamond necklace becomes the diamond garrote. A beautiful corpse, but ravaged. Anarchism is mold thriving on a carcass. *Sola fide, sola gratia.* Belief is weeds.

PURITY OF HEART IS TO WILL ONE THING

And Moses said unto him, Enviest thou for my sake? would God that all the LORD's people were prophets, *and* that the LORD would put his spirit upon them!

—Numbers 11:29

But I did end up back at the hated apartment complex, despite my declaration to Liz on the day of the raid. I went back, one last visit, a postscript, to retrieve something from my old life that actually had use value apart from what it could be sold for: my bicycle.

It was astonishing, really, that I had forgotten to take it before. I felt stupid, careless, and prayed the whole walk over that I wouldn't find it stolen or stripped. *Parker, please grant me this bicycle, that I may use it to bring glory to Your Name and spread Your Word.*

It was right where I had left it—a silver road bike with wide-tread tires. Hallelujah! It didn't even need to be taken in for air.

Back home—it was September—I stood before the broken bedroom mirror and stared at my face. I had a hole in my beard. It was a small spot, say half a dime's width, where nothing grew but a few stunted, forked-end hairs. In all my years as a daily shaver, I had never known nor so much as suspected that there was this barren, blasted region in the landscape of my face. Now my beard flowed wild, black, curly, and thick, grown out and growing still. I loved to play with it, as did my lovers. It felt especially good to be patted, an upward motion from below that made the beard coil like mattress springs. A welcome pressure. Hair grew high up on my cheeks, my sideburns bushed out, wisps curling back around napeward. My mustache spilled over my lip. And actually, you couldn't see the beard bald spot, which was on the underside of my chin, a secret tunnel. Sometimes I would take a finger and slide it into the hole, where it was humid, somehow cavernous and close at once, the way the tongue perceives a gap between two teeth. Fascinated by this, I restlessly touched and touched, worried those stunted hairs until they fell loose and the hidden skin grew irritated and flaked. *This is who you are,* I thought, and my eyes were wet with love for myself and my lovers and for the world.

How wonderful and strange it is to be alive! How uneven we are, and how lucky, in our delirious specificity and holy broken forms. Since moving into Fishgut I had made self-discovery into a full-fledged occupation, into a perpetual act of devotion. I understood my body, and the bodies around me, not merely as "bodies" in the abstract but as the bodies that they, individually, actually were. And the souls that those bodies housed, and how soul and body worked in concert, happily bound. I pressed down on Katy's clitoris like ringing the doorbell of her spirit, and when it answered the door I gave it a sloppy wet kiss. We were all in love with each other all the time, world without end in its endless perfecting and eternal imperfection, God never grant us permanence, for perfection equals stasis equals death, only ever revolution forever, amen.

I fletched, loaded, fired the arrow that pierces the cloud of unknowing. I rode my bicycle all over campus, up crowded walking paths and across green quads, through parking lots, skirting shrubbery and fountains, jumping curbs, a celebrant, thinking, *Every moment of freedom is glory unto God's name*; thinking, *I can go even faster than this if I want to*; thinking, *You sad sheep, how unlike you I am; I, the rider of the silver bike, I the holy goat.*

Around Lake Alice, where turtle heads peep from murkwater and tame gators laze on the shore. Past the nondenominational meditation center (a lakeview pavilion with stained glass; available for weddings, etc.; inquire for rates). Past the acres of student garden plots by the plant science buildings, where I had encouraged Anchor to make at least some use of the fact she was still a student and take an elective that might teach her organic gardening which would be essential after the country's infrastructure collapsed—when the good times came—but she, selfishly, had chosen a creative writing course instead. A small softball diamond and bleachers, side by side with a soccer field. A water purification plant that stank like eggs. The Harn Museum of Art. Still more outbuildings and open spaces of indeterminate university function. Eventually, depending which way I went, I exited the campus to find my-self either on Archer Road or on Thirty-fourth Street—each a miserable strip of fast-food chains and big-box stores, Block-busters and Office Depots, Ruby Tuesdays and Olive Gar-dens. Ah, glory of the free market! Ah, surfeit of choice!

I liked taking Archer because it hooks back around the south side of campus, past the Beaty Towers, and meets up with Thirteenth Street, one of the border roads of the student ghetto, which I could take nearly all the way home. Or, if I took Thirteenth the *other* way, I could ride out to Paynes Prairie, the so-called Alachua Savannah, where you could glimpse horse herds and buffalo at sunrise and evening, and the walking trails were dotted with signs warning of wild boar. It was to this prehistoric place that Parker had fled, like John the Baptist in the wilderness, I imagined. I could *see* him out there, how his presence was like a bolt of pure spirit-lightning streaking through the sweep of God's untroubled creation, how scope is its own wisdom, how truth is the only thing that lasts.

But I saw construction sites also. Not on the prairie, of course—which was a protected nature preserve—but on the long road leading to it, as well as all throughout town. More and more always, single-family homes demolished, stands of trees cut down. They were making way for apartment com-plexes like the one I had lived in. Everywhere I went I saw the cancer, the devastation, as Parker himself had seen it, and my heart was sick to look upon these things, and I wanted to somehow get involved, not stand apart and watch. But what would I do? Join some group? Write a letter? Paint a sign and hold it up? *Let the dead bury the dead*, I thought. *Let the world solve the problem of the world.*

Our house became a beacon, even as the other houses on our block were emptied out, went dark. Consolidated Properties was moving in like the land sharks they were, but our man Stuckins stuck fast, and our autonomous zone was safe and we were safe inside it; indeed we were flourishing, a desert orchid in flower, as up and down the block buyout prices were reached, and the street became such a ghost town there might as well have been tumbleweeds.

There was nobody left to call in noise complaints on us and we rejoiced in the awesome power of the Lord.

Word spread of us, rumors of what we preached and who we were. People wanted to see and to know. We were sought out. Our travelers' rest was full now, and Thomas's old room, which had become another one, was, too. We were a hostel, sort of, but that was only the beginning of what we were. There were a dozen people living at Fishgut—auspicious number!—and numbers untold passing through and dropping in. It was not unusual at any given hour to see one or a few punks in contemplative silence or loud slurred professions of devotion about Parker's shrine. Services ran every Sunday night now and were followed by staple-and-fold sessions. Copies of the Good Zine were stacked up in piles, slipped into newspaper machines, stuffed into the backpacks of our departing guests. They left with as many as we could copy, as many as they had space to take. All bound for distribution—anywhere, everywhere, wherever. Our book was dandelion fluff; windborne spore. Our devotion was repaid a thousandfold. People brought us or sent us all kinds of things we never asked for: money, gifts, whatever they had. We always had more than we needed, and gave as much as we could of it away again—to our congregants, the local homeless, curious college kids who happened by. We were a small blazing light in the distance on a darkling plain. We were a mystery cult, attuned to the necessity of eternal pursuit, perpetual perfecting, and the violent, transformative Grace of our lawless God.

Winning converts. Like the door guy at Clasen's, Shrike was his name; a veteran scenester who did tattoos. We could get into shows for free now, and he brought his equipment over on Sunday nights when he wasn't working, and during the reveries that followed our services he offered up Parker's Mark at ink cost to anyone who felt themselves ready. The labor itself he gave out of love. I took a big swig of something clear that burned my throat, handed the bottle off to someone, and got in Shrike's line. He was sitting on a small stool he'd brought. I sat in Katy's favorite chair.

I am a book, I remember thinking, as the needle seethed over my flesh—my teeth clenched and *Lord give me strength* my eyes shut tightly and trying not to jerk away or wince too much—*I am a book and this is my inscription. I am dedicated now and for all time.*

We circled round the hate-breathing evangelists who haunted Turlington Plaza, a large outdoor gathering place on campus, who shouted about hellfire and chastity and faggots and otherwise made a brutal spectacle of their miscarriage of God's love. They stood in the lumpy shadow of a great gray-brown abstract sculpture that everyone called the Potato. It was ringed by wooden benches and you weren't supposed to climb it, but you could, and some of us did, while others gathered close, cinching the preachers in our snare—whoever it was on that day, whichever denomination, the exact ones changed. A Baptist sweating through a cheap suit, a Chinese Adventist in an ankle-length dress with long sleeves, a suited-up Witness with an armload of pamphlets not so different, in the end, from our own. Being wrongly dressed for the weather seemed essential to all of their programs. From wherever we were—up above him, all around her—we raised our voices and preached back, louder: the good gospel of anarchy in a raucous eruption of joyful noise. There we were, Legion-like, earnest and bonkers in torn tee shirts and paint-spattered shorts, louder and more interesting than whatever it was we were disrupting, a source of endless envy and nuisance to the straitjacketed, sad-eyed world.

At night, in the rooftop pool of the hotel across from campus, doing cannonballs or diving down and hugging bottom till our chests burned, thinking *The body is the site of all experience in this world,* swimming up against some other body, *Now we see each other face to face,* a hand reaching for the slippery neck of a bottle, *Joy is a better form of prayer than prayer,* playing chicken or running where you weren't supposed to, bright flashes of pale flesh in moonlight—see we weren't always serious, and knew how to have fun like kids do, like everyone should, like humans were made and meant to: exultant, dirty innocence; hellbent pleasure; Zerowork. The biggest, hairiest kids you ever saw.

We spread out across town—paired off or by our lonesomes or in freewheeling squads—to open dumpsters and the unalarmed back doors of stores. We barely distinguished between products and trash any longer—there was only what we needed or wanted or could get. If it was available, our opinion of its worth was no longer a relevant consideration, or, better put: availability itself was a strange attractor and bestowed value, Midas-like, on all that it touched.

When the thefts, scroungings, and donations yielded more than we knew what to do with—four toasters, ten lamps!—we held yard "sales," great giveaways, where everything was free. We stapled fliers to utility poles and filled our front yard up with stuff. Little old lady bargain seekers turned dumpstered serving plates upside down in the vain search for a price tag. "Just take it," we said. "It's yours." A deal, and they would have been happy. But free? They only stared at us, lips

pursed in grim suspicion, both hands clutching the pocket-
book, looking us up and down. "I'll have to think about it,"
they said, and walked away; wary glances back over slumped
shoulders—what did we care? We had done our best by
them. Anything we couldn't get rid of we gleefully destroyed,
and made raw materials of the gleaming rubble—splintered
wood and glass chips, perfect for bricolage, for conceptual
sculpture! Whatever anyone wanted or could dream up, and
this is not to suggest that the generative acts of destruction
weren't regarded as artistic expressions in and of themselves.

There were only a few things we found impossible to forage
for or steal: hard liquor, illegal drugs, the rent, and photo-
copies. At the Bullseye Copy Center on Thirteenth Street
they trusted you to keep your own count, and so you could
lowball the final figure easily by half, even three quarters,
and the cashier wasn't going to argue; he wasn't getting paid
enough to care. These few facts of life were all that kept us
contributing to the American imperium and its blood economy—these plus the modest costs associated with the house
itself, electricity for example, but we were working on cracking the power meter. Nothing had availed yet, but that didn't
mean that nothing would.

We kept a General Fund, to which all contributed as
they could. There were three main ways to raise money—by
stealing things from chain stores and then returning those
items to other locations of the same chain, by busking for
change in the streets (this was the riskiest, as well as the least

effective; nobody's less generous than college students), or by "donating" blood plasma for cash.

We prayed over the money orders we sent to pay the rent and other bills before we mailed them, and for the spirits of whoever was going that week to The Life You Save—that was the plasma center's name—*Lord and Parker, we lament the sin of this our participation in the system.* They were prayers of apology, but not, note, pleas for forgiveness. That would have been madness, naturally, since we knew from the teachings of our own Good Zine that God held us in no soul debt; our devotion to Him was given freely, as His love was to us. We owed Him nothing.

I rode down University Avenue to the strip mall at the corner of Sixth Street. It was a short enough ride but afforded me a clear view the whole time of the Seagle Building, which I would have rather not had. Whenever I saw that shape, that white blot on the blue horizon, my mind flashed to thoughts of my old life, my dead life, pre-life, life of living death—computer warmth, rented furniture, flawless carpet, office light. It took everything I had to shut these images out. *Purity of heart is to will one thing,* I thought.

What was the one thing that I willed?

Everything.

The one thing I wanted was it all.

The strip mall was run-down, six or seven storefronts, mostly vacant, with a parking lot that could have held a hundred cars and hardly ever held ten. The asphalt was sun-savaged and weed-choked, white-gray and fissured, jagged chunks of stone upturned or missing. I dismounted the bike and walked it.

The mall boasted exactly two operational businesses. The first was a locally owned office supply store that struggled, but so far had held on, against Office Depot, Walmart, and all the rest. The second business was The Life You Save.

I was led to a small white cubicle in a big white room and told to sit down on a strip of butcher paper, in a chair like at the dentist. They had my information in the file already—this was not my first visit—and so certain preliminaries were dispensed with. We skipped straight to the questions about developments in my personal life. Were there any new additions since the last visit to my track record of sexual partners, intravenous drug use, or tattoos? The still-tender skin on my chest tingled and buzzed as I lied to the attendant—over the right breast, exactly opposite my heart—and as the sensation increased in intensity I became certain that Parker's Mark was actually lit up on my body, my sacred heart aflame and shining through the thin fabric of my plain black tee shirt, announcing my true faith to the world.

This idea was so powerful that I actually glanced—quickly, furtively, worried they'd notice—down at my chest. I was only slightly disappointed to see that there was no light there. But at least I was able to put the weird notion to rest and finish giving the attendant the answers she wanted, that we both needed ("no, nothing new to report") in order to get her to recline the chair, hook me up to the boxy white machine.

The attendant was a middle-aged black woman with her mind on something else. She wore pale pink scrubs, a nurse uniform, though she wasn't a nurse. She did the first arm all right but couldn't find the vein on my other arm. I'd thought that after the tattoo, one prick ought to be a breeze for me, but it turned out that I really just didn't like needles, or pain, period. The third time she stuck me I let a little startled whimper escape, and that was the time she finally nailed the target, as if my crying out had been an essential step in the process. She flipped a switch and the machine buzzed awake. She messed with knobs, set levels, then said she'd be back to check on me in about an hour. I shut my eyes against the fluorescent battery above, the miserable office-white wash, tried to slink into the deep and original soul-self, as my blood slunk out of my body and into the white machine that no longer buzzed but now, working, clunked and hummed. I called up into my mind the image of Parker's Book—not the Good Zine, now, but the original, the Mead—and saw its cover open and its pages fan, and recited lines to myself from memory and meditated upon their true meanings' flowering forth.

Let our lives be our politics and not our politics our lives.

This was just a warm-up, really. The line was clear, direct, and applicable presently. My drained blood was spun apart in a centrifuge. The plasma was separated out and collected—yellow, transparent, gelid—in an IV bag that hung from a pole that jutted up from the machine. When the not-nurse returned she would collect the bag and take it for flash-freezing, and in that paused form it would enter the global capitalist economy, sold and resold on private markets by specialty brokers who kept their identities concealed, until finally it ended up in some research lab, or a Japanese hospital, or who the hell knew. The blood was pumped back into my body through my other arm. What they gave back was depleted, a nearly waterless slurry of cells. For letting them do this they would give me forty dollars. I was a hypocrite today, pimped out to them, but this small compromise of my values was part of the larger work of preserving them the rest of the time, and so in a certain sense no compromise at all, and here seemed to be the crux of it, the heart of the paradox, paradox as the thumping heart of the living prospect—thumping like my own heart thumped, as the white machine sucked like an undertow and my red life darkened the clear thin tubes.

He stood at the foot of my chair and was smiling at me. He was taller than I was, but I wasn't sure by how much. Half a foot, perhaps. It was hard to tell, and also seemed, sometimes, to change. He wore cleanish blue jeans gone to shreds at the ankles and a plain black tee shirt like mine. He was barefoot. At his neck he wore a small, tasteful silver cross on a black cord—not quite a choker, but close. I could not describe his face, though I saw it perfectly clearly.

"All this," I said, and gestured with my head at my splayed, cathetered arms, "is for your glory."

"I know," he said. "You're doing really good."

"We pray and wait, Parker. We pray so hard."

"Keep it up," he said. "Desire is a strange attractor. But you know that already. Now listen to what I'm about to tell you."

"Yes, Parker."

"This machine infuses your blood with something called citrate, which keeps it from clotting inside the lines. It does this by binding to calcium, so when you finish here you should find a tall glass of milk, or an ice cream cone. If you can't steal any, take a few bucks out of the General Fund."

"Are you sure? What if somebody asks me about it?" He had admonished me not to tell the others about our conversations. These visions were personal, and private, he'd said—a secret, and when I asked him why, he would say only that the reason for the secret was a secret, too.

"They won't ask. It'll be okay."

"Thank you," I said. "All glory be to your name."

"Not my name, but the one who named us. Our souls are our names," Parker said. "You already know this. Every moment of our living is us hearing God speak our names, and our listening to him speak is us knowing ourselves."

The not-nurse stuck her head into the cubicle, the little not-quite room.

"Doin' okay?" she said.

"Better than just okay," I replied. She shrugged—what was it to her?

"Okay then," she said. "I come back in another half hour and unhook you."

She went away and I looked back to where Parker had been, knowing he would no longer be there, but hoping anyway, then sinking into disappointment, then berating myself for that disappointment, because I knew how he would have despised it. I should have been grateful he had come at all.

I was light-headed now. My thoughts were drifting; they floated easy over the past few months, which laid themselves out before me, like a landscape painting. Through Parker's grace I had been given the boon of Sight, and as I lay back in my chair, I allowed my body's eyes to shut, slowed my breathing down, so to let the eyes of my heart blink open, and my spirit dreamed expansively beyond its gilded cage of flesh. *Even in this moment,* I thought, *I can hear God speaking my name!* I saw scenes and visions of those whom I loved.

I saw Thomas in his adopted home, Seattle, holding a black laundry marker, writing the number of the free legal aid hotline upside down on his stomach, so that later, after he got arrested during a protest and had all his belongings taken, he'd be able to simply lift his shirt and know who to call.

I was seeing the future, I realized. I was seeing the shape of things to come.

Owl and Selah at the New Year's Eve camp-out concert in Big Cypress, way down south, which that goofy band Phish was throwing. For all Owl's talk about Asheville, old friends,

and new prospects, everyone who knew them knew they would
go the other way, farther down into the cul-de-sac of Florida,
and drink mushroom tea with their fellow travelers and worship nonsense and noodly guitar. Somebody's toddler running
wild through the crowd, all the legs like a forest to him.

I saw Anchor at home in her dorm room—could this
be the present now?—stretched out on her belly across her
unmade twin bed. There was a Bob Marley poster on the
wall on the roommate's side. Anchor's own wall was bare,
her socked feet bobbing in the air as she composed a poem
for her creative writing class.

Song

We stand apart and are beautiful
Even when most ugly. We are furious
With anything that hums, clanks—how
Many greasy gears have ground us down,
Axled dumb as the sun to the years?

We say better destroyed by
Than to become; better die
In opposition than live mastered.
We love to fertilize: each
Unto each and all, in time, the grasses.

The worst injustice is being named
For what we stand ever against

And standing ever against it, ever fall.
We are originals. The world has lost
Its way and you know what we mean.

You don't prefer, indeed refuse
To hear first principles and origin
Myths. Neither the screaming
Nor the stifled screaming
Of your victims and constituents.

Nobody builds us monuments. We lose
No faith, no war, only blood and battles.
We prove Grace, and the limits of Grace.
Together alone is our true song ever sung.
We were old when the world was young.

I thought that was a pretty good poem—but of course it wasn't really Anchor's. It was my own creation. I had made it up from the strength of my vision of her. My love for the truth and for my friends was so strong that even as she pulled away from us I could see her more clearly in my mind, as though she sat right across the room from me, as if she stood as close to me as Parker had only moments ago.

But I was confused by my poem. I didn't understand what I had meant by "most ugly." By "the limits of Grace." Ugliness, after all, was impossible in a world where all was permitted and beautiful, constituted by the fact of its inherent Grace, which was—would be—unending. But perhaps I had simply meant something about the way in which Grace manifests, or is bestowed. It was worth thinking about. I was teaching myself, it seemed, or wasn't it possible that Parker was speaking through me? That the eruption of these verses was a reverberation, an aftereffect, an echo, of the gift of his having come? But what if I were to forget the poem? I needed to preserve it! If I were to call out for a pen and paper, would the plasma people bring me these things? Could I commit my poem to memory? I would finally have something of my own to share at the open mic! But then I thought how *Desire is a strange attractor. Your longing warps the arc of the world's emergent truth* and I saw that Parker had come to show me something, if I would only have ears to hear him and eyes to see. Strange attractor, yes. My desire as right action in the world. I would not write the poem down, but instead concentrate all my spirit on the vision in my mind of Anchor writing it. By the sheer force of *my* longing, she would compose it herself.

The knife edge of heat dulled even as the greens of the trees did—we had cooling, and then cool, and then cold rain, and didn't break in anymore to the hotel pool—and the days grew short, and shadows lengthened. November came and we switched the clocks back. The snowbird-punks began to appear. These were a strange breed, reverse jet-setters, people who'd been living outside or in raw squats all around the Northeast and were now looking to scout new homes in warmer climates, spend their winters bumming around the snowless

South. I can't say who came and went when, exactly, but I can picture all of their upturned faces—smudged with dirt, or else fresh after a grateful turn in our shower—while Katy and I sermonized. I remember dumpster runs they helped us with, or things we talked about sitting around the living room: how it would be after the state fell and we lived in the eternal revolution and walked with God, or nights they spent in our six or four or two or ten arms. I remember only fragments of their stories, or else fragments were all I ever knew.

Dennis was a pro-bicycle, anti-car activist from Arizona. He taught us how to fix and replace our own brakes and gears.

Heidi, a German girl touring the States on her gap year. An astonishing blonde, for whom Aaron fell hard. She took him to hop his first train and they made it as far as Louisiana, where they got arrested for skinny-dipping in a private pool, trying to soothe nasty doses of poison ivy they'd picked up in a hobo jungle in Alabama, waiting for a train. They explained about the poison ivy to the cop who busted them (leaving out the part about the train) but he misheard what they said and by the time they went before the judge for trespassing two days later it was generally known about the precinct and the courthouse that both the hobos had HIV. The backwater judge threw their charges out on the condition that they get straight out of town—he didn't want that kind of shit in his district, not even locked up. Was this not an example of God's abundant grace? Aaron came home; I don't know where the girl went next.

Jackie Jazz—so many of them named themselves!—wore a porkpie hat that was no less dashing for how bad it smelled, and traveled with his best friend, a mongrel dog (about which, ditto).

Byron was a black secessionist. He believed that if the South had won the Civil War, the institution of slavery would have inevitably collapsed in short order, and that this sea change would have spread to the white working classes as well, triggering a socialistic awakening throughout the whole region. Without the humiliation of defeat and the economic colonialism of the Northern carpetbagging industrialists, the whole modern history of Southern race relations would have been entirely different, trending toward a universal equality that would have by now been long since achieved. No miscegenation laws, no lynchings, no separate but equal, no Jim Crow. Plus, a defeated and weakened North would never have managed to complete their seizure of the American continent, or even to hold on to what they had. Byron sported a Confederate flag on his guitar case and held in his head an alternate map of the country, where the Southwest was part of Mexico, the Northwest was a sovereign unified Indian nation, California was the Bear Flag Republic, the Northeast was something like Eastern Europe, and we all lived in the Socialist Confederacy, which thrived. Moreover, in this formulation, there would have been no American Empire to replace the already-ailing British one, and the entire Age of Empires would have hastened all the more rapidly toward its end. So really, he said, the whole world would have been different, and better, if only the South had triumphed. Was this really so wild a notion? We begged him to start over from the beginning; take us through it again.

Paolo brought his own tent and pitched it in the side yard—the *other* side—between the far end of the house and the chain-link fence, a weedy lane where nobody ever went. Paolo had a thick black head of hair spilling out from beneath a Florida Gators ballcap that might have been ironic, earnest, or just the first thing he'd grabbed. He was short, five three maybe, with a narrow, almost girlish waist, but there was nothing else feminine about him. He was fatless, compact rather than petite, and when he walked around with his shirt off (a nature kid, he usually did) it was impossible not to pause in whatever you were doing, swept up in gawking admiration of this specimen of optimum design. His body was hypnotic, his movements leopardlike, every muscle stood out in relief beneath his olive-gold skin. He could scramble ten feet straight up the trunk of a tree. Katy spent nights out in the tent with him, sometimes, but never did coax him into our room. Or maybe, I thought sometimes, she never tried.

Todd was an ecstasy freak who loved trancey jam bands. He rolled into town following the Disco Biscuits on their Southeast run, met Owl out in front of the library downtown, where they were both busking, and came back to the house with him so they could trade Dead tapes. He liked it at Fishgut so much he decided to skip the Tampa-Orlando-Miami leg of the tour, and we spent the next week so stoned we couldn't speak—his pot had been dusted with something, but he never said what—and then one day some buddies of his came by in a beat-up station wagon with bug dots all over the windshield and a bumper sticker that said TREY IS A JEDI (we didn't ask). He left, but took with him an entire box of Good Zines, and promised to distribute them over the next leg of the Biscuits' tour: a three-night stand at a club in Athens, and then points north. He and his buddies had a little gas grill and were planning to pay their way selling grilled-cheese sandwiches (as well as a few sheets of acid) in the parking lots outside the shows. We reminded him the Zines were never—ever—to be sold, only given away freely. It was printed right there on the cover. Did he see? "Yeah, man, yeah," he said. "I get it. I'll give one away with every purchase—how's that?" Good enough, or it would have to be. They left.

All these places, names of cities, train routes and state lines and destinations and rendezvouses. I didn't *believe* in them. They explained the movements of bodies through space, sure, their passage in and out of view—Aaron gone, then an interval, then here again—but ultimately, what were they except useful fictions? Fishgut was what was real to me. The house was a planet, the city the solar system in which we spun. These people, travelers, always sounded so tiny when they described their movements across the country or the world, like grains of rice skittering in an oil drum. Those of us who stayed, who were the unwavering center, the rock-solid core of the house, saw that they suffered from a reversal of perspective, one that impeded their spiritual progress. The world was within us, every *person* a planet and the *house* the solar system, and the city—I don't know, not the universe exactly; maybe Gainesville was the sun. Parker spoke of Gainesvilles flung out across the country like stars in the night, and what was the sun but a star? For us there was only here, plus wherever Parker was, which could have been anywhere and so was essentially nowhere. So there was Here and not-Here. And when he returned to us there would be Here alone.

Cassidy and Robot had been married in some sort of pagan ritual that the state didn't recognize, which was fitting, they said, since they themselves did not recognize the state. They had a toddler with them, a bright-eyed and slightly underfed boy named Lincoln, for the place where he had been conceived, on the very day that the two had met at a Greyhound station. They had come down to Florida for a Rainbow Gathering, and had been wed in the forest, with the tree sprites and tripping hippies all bearing happy witness, but their ride had left without them and now they were adrift.

"You wouldn't believe how hard it is hitching with three people," Cassidy said. "If it was just me and the kid, it might be easy—people take pity on a woman in trouble. A single mom, you know. But with him"—she forked a thumb at Robot and clucked her tongue—"forget it."

"You never gettin' rid of me, baby," Robot said to her, grinning. Cassidy grinned back at him. She was trying to fix her ratty hair up in a bun.

"Don't I know it, baby?" she shot back, and then they both broke up laughing like this was just the funniest thing. Couples.

They were on opposite sides of the living room. It was late. Who knew what time, exactly, and what did it matter? We were working our way through the last of Todd's parting gift to us—two blunts rolled with that mystery weed—and everyone was pretty much zonked. Katy was in her favorite chair, holding Lincoln and bouncing him on her lap. I was on my knees on the floor in front of the chair, eye level with the kid, making silly faces at him so he laughed and clapped his hands, each slap of his palms filling the air with showers of silver light like sparklers make. And the faces I made at Lincoln were making Katy laugh, too, and when she laughed I could see her aura brighten, and I wondered what she would look like if she laughed forever, which was an absurd thought, actually nightmarish in its way. Wasn't there something neurotic about the entire concept of the eternal? This had never occurred to me before. The thought was a sudden alien, absurd, and far too much to wrap my head around; it spooked me badly, but then my perception of its absurdity began to seem like the thing that was truly absurd, and the meta-absurdity of *that* sort of shoved the absurdity proper out of the way, and in the course of think-watch-feeling all of this happen inside my head—while still, the whole time, goggling at the baby, to his continuing amusement—I realized that I was way more fucked-up than I had thought I was, and maybe shouldn't actually be around a child—and I looked around the room and wondered who else this might be true of, umm everyone, and thought: who *were* all these people, these people who were us, who were sitting around pickled to the gills on whatever day of the week this was and why hadn't we made sure the child got to bed on time—not that he or we had anything in particular to be up for the next day, but wasn't there like a general idea out there that kids should get their rest? The breadth and depth of God's trust in us seemed in this moment so vast as to be crushing, suffocating—or else, the more terrifying thought, *it was entirely absent*, there was no God and He had no trust to place in us, and we were just there, alone, fuck-ups and dropouts playing in the sandbox of our own tinfoil-hat ideas, while the kid's parents had their bottom-shelf love affair and the kid himself was probably not getting enough vitamins or exercise, was going to grow up chunky, with short, weak bones.

The man who said, "Lord, make my faith stronger" was already a believer.

I had stopped making faces at the baby—moments or minutes ago, I had no idea. Hot, silent tears ran down my face, which Lincoln reached out to touch, and Katy no doubt assumed that these were tears of joy (I had become, in my advancing faith, rather prone to crying jags) so she held him forward so that he could. Small grubby fingers played across my wet cheeks, then down, where they found my beard and, fascinated, grasped then gave a little tug. "God is love," I said, in a voice that sounded strange to my own ears. I sounded as if I were defending a position in an argument, rather than simply stating a fact. And I had shouted at the kid, who was staring at me in stunned silence, perhaps about to cry himself. I wriggled free of his little hand and stood up. My knees ached. How long had I been kneeling, frozen in the bodily grammar of supplication, the soul-seared plea? I walked out of the living room, reminding myself that we all experience paroxysms of doubt from time to time, and that the struggle to believe only made my faith stronger. Perhaps, at some level, if considered in this way, I *had* in fact been crying tears of joy.

In the kitchen, I filled a tall glass of water from the sink, drank it all, then poured another. With this second glass in hand, I meant to return to the living room. I was almost sure that nobody besides Katy had seen me crying, or had any inkling at all of what had gone on. Only she had witnessed my disturbance, and so it was not surprising that when I turned around she was standing in the doorway of the kitchen, and without speaking gestured toward our room. The child was back in the care of its wasted mother. I followed my lover down the short length of our hall. Both guest rooms had their doors cracked; light and noise spilled from one, darkness and quiet abided in the other. Whatever anyone wants or desires. Everything, anything, all the time. Our room was dark. No candles were lit. The bed was empty. I sat down, facing myself in our broken mirror. Katy stepped between me and it.

"Where's Anchor?" I asked.

"I don't know. Why?"

"She should be here. Why did she help us make the Zine if she wasn't going to ever be here?"

"I don't know."

"She wrote a poem but she won't show it to me because she can't accept what it says."

"Did you ask to see it?"

"How could I? She hasn't *been* here."

"Then how do you know she wrote it?"

"I saw her."

"David, what are you talking about? You can tell me."

But I couldn't. Parker was behind her, looking out at me from within the mirror, his visage sharded and off-angled by the forking cracks. His wings were folded up but I could see them trembling. He was giving me a meaningful look. So I just said, "I'm sorry. I guess I'm pretty fucked-up. Like, stoned, I mean, but Anchor is supposed to be one of us. We *need* her. That's all."

"Well, you know I'd like that, too, but it's really up to Anchor."

"The truth moves through her but she denies it."

"I still don't know what you mean, but if so, that's her own choice. I think you should sleep, David."

"I want to take a walk, I think."

"I wish you'd stay here."

"No, it'll be good for me. It'll clear my head. *Please.*"

"You don't need my permission, David, for this or for anything."

"I know that, but I still want it. Will you just say it for me?"

"I don't want to."

"Just this once."

Her lips twisted into a grimace, her eyes cast down, me waiting as she weighed the absolute force of my need against the equal and opposite force of her beliefs, our shared faith, which stated that no one had power over any other, so how could permission ever be given, if authority was not held? I had no right to ask this thing of her, but her love for me was without limits, was the constitutive fact of the world even as the founding gesture of law always must lie outside the system of law that it establishes, which is why there is no such thing as legitimate law of any kind.

"Okay," she said, her voice slivered and raw. For the sake of my love she sinned. I kissed her lips, which did not open for me or move at all; she was a figure of infinite resignation, and received my sin into herself. I brushed past her and out of the bedroom, the kitchen door, the backyard, the house. I left. It was easy, really. I just disappeared into the dark.

Where was our prophet, and why did he not come?

He could not, I reasoned, have been waylaid or detained. And so I began to wonder if it was us ourselves, somehow, who delayed him. Wherever he was, and even as by his Grace I saw visions and into hearts, so he saw us, into our hearts, and there was something that displeased him, or anyway, gave him pause. He would return when we were worthy—I mean ready, I guess; it's hard to keep the language straight so you are really saying what you mean. Worthiness of course is tied to hierarchy, standards, ratings, merit, and so could not have possibly been what I meant.

Where was Parker right now? Like, where was he *actually in the world*? Was he still in the state of Florida? In Alachua County? Had he left us (them) to return to the Prairie—was he a pile of swamp bones? Or was he truly Elsewhere? Squatting in Alphabet City with some new crew of wild boys, or a Krishna now, or a Trappist monk. Or had his spirit finally blown like an old tire or an eardrum, so that the voice of God was as silence to him? Did he work a straight job—the night shift at some gas station in southeast Texas? A father-to-be in Carson City? Was he headed to Seattle himself, and would he march in the Black Bloc with Thomas, brave through clouds of tear gas, and would their streaming red eyes peek out from the thin smiles in their balaclavas, and would those gazes catch in the midst of the crush, amid bodies and swung batons and concussion grenades, and would they see one another face to face, as if in Heaven, and if they did then so what?

How old was Parker?

Had he turned thirty yet?

Was his hair grown thin?

Was he with Terry?

Terry and Terry and Terry. He or she and who. Who was this person with whom Parker had traveled through the Badlands—and who knew where they had been before that, or where they had gone after. Who *was* Terry? Male or female? Lover of Parker's, or friend? The entry was undated, and even Katy didn't know who Terry was. Parker had never mentioned any Terry; so far as she knew he had had no friends but her and Thomas—even Liz had had to admit that she'd barely known him. There was more to Parker's life than the Book recorded. That much was to be expected. But the idea of this Terry—of Terry's tremendous effect on our Parker—arrested my attention and disturbed my mind. I had argued against including the Terry section in the Good Zine, but Katy had insisted. In fact, on the point of this particular passage, Katy's and my respective positions had been inverted—we switched sides.

> Every college town is heaven, each one different but the same, like hoboing from Gainesville to Gainesville to Gainesville, a hundred Gainesvilles flung across the country, like stars in the sky.

"This is the heart of it, right?" I had said to Katy, hoping that if I threw her own words back at her she would have to accede. But Katy wanted to include the whole entry; that Parker was capable of receiving and giving love, that he was willing to open himself to—that he was even capable of—intimacy on strictly human terms ("That's it") seemed to fully realize him for her. He was all too human as much as he was all too holy, and this vision of double excess was for her the highest manifestation of Parker's own notion of the joyful paradox, the conscious dwelling in the mystery of the heart and the heart of mystery. She saw in the Terry episode a validation of our (or was it really just her?) particular interpretation of Parker's teachings. This text was the essence of the Book, she said, essential to include, and she had been willing to trade me any passage I wanted in exchange for my backing down. And so she got to include Terry, and I got to include the meditation on the Kierkegaard quote, which she had been pushing to cut.

The Book is in the world to be read by the world.

When you read the Book the Book reads you back.

The Book multiplies the Book.

What is there to do in the world but read the Book?

And be read by the Book in turn.

Anarchism allows for the notion of Legitimate Authority. After the Revolution, even though everything will be different and more honest and better, we won't make the Soviet mistake of pulling jobs out of hats so that electricians are doing surgery and chefs are fitting pipe. Parker was a Legitimate Authority, which was why we spread his ideals and followed his model, antimodel though it was. But being against all authority, even his own, he would necessarily wish to redistribute that knowledge—this is what we were doing for him with the Good Zine—so that his own Legitimate Authority would no longer be required, or else would be indistinguishable from the equally legitimate authority of everyone else. Was it possible then that it was our yearning itself that delayed him? Was the force of our longing acting as a barrier instead of a draw? Perhaps he would only return to us when he himself was no longer necessary, when he could stand in the Fishgut dooryard and declare, "Behold, I am your prophet!" and have us answer him in one voice, "We are all prophets here!"

Or was *that* heresy?

And if so was it necessarily a problem? Could heresy possibly be the point?

What was he trying, in the pressing weight of his absence, to show us and why were we failing so utterly *to see*?

I could feel every eye upon me as I entered Clasen's. Even the ones looking away had me in their attention. All the cliques and subcliques. Skinny girls, deathpale, with short black bangs and star tattoos; activist kids with red bandanas tied loose at their bearded necks. To some of the people here I was, no doubt, a legend. To others, doubtless too, a lunatic, part of the filthy insurgent faction that had forced a gaping split in the scene. Such limited vision, these people—no sense of gravity; no *scope*. But they were yet all of them right—paradox, faith, mystery—for Parker preached Right Action, even as before him Christ had foretold that brother would turn against brother, because the Word He had brought them was a sword.

I was hungry, but the guy working the counter wasn't one of Ours. Later I would stick my hand in the garbage, see what some wasteful punks had failed to finish and likewise failed to save. These people who thought that they were better, who believed that they were already living the truth of their ideals!

I wove my way through the crowd to the back room, where there was a second and denser press. I was just in time for the headline act, who were working their way through the audience ahead of me, because Clasen's had no greenroom, no backstage at all. I heard a guy in front of me tell his friend that the next band was called the Dust Biters, and that they played folk songs, but like *differently*.

The band was only two guys: a drummer and a guitar player. The drum kit was homemade, paint cans and gray plastic buckets; one golden Zildjian cymbal the only object in the setup serving the purpose for which it had been made. The singer wore clean black jeans and a black tee shirt, like mine and Parker's. He was pasty-pale and had close-cropped brown hair. A generic, guy-looking guy. He seemed nervous and kept his gaze fixed on the acoustic-electric guitar he held, first because he was tuning it, and then after just to have somewhere to look. The drummer knocked off a few rolls, then did a rim shot. We, the crowd, hushed. The singer looked up at us, then turned back to face the drummer. If they exchanged words, we didn't hear them. The singer nodded, then turned back to us, but seemed not to see us now. His lips brushed up against the microphone, and a woolly swoosh swept over the room.

"Fuck Bob Dylan," he said quietly, then struck a chord so loud my knees actually buckled, and the drummer followed like hell on his heels and the room dissolved into a marvelous frenzy of limbs and sweat and noise, and my body was swept up and I felt freed of myself, like my soul was loose, and I rose up to the ceiling of that sweltering room and looked down at all of us, and saw my head whip and body flail as I moved toward the center of the gyre, where the big punks were spinning like planets and colliding like tectonic plates, I was crushed and nearly trampled but then quick hands slid under my arms and lifted me—I did not feel these things, *I saw them*—I went to my feet again, then higher still, dozens of hands on my body, lifting me till I rose to the top of the crowd and they held me aloft and passed me around, I was inches from the old pressed-tin ceiling, my arms thrust out like Christ's and my eyes shut tight, rolling on the surface of the fray, and in the midst of this ecstasy I heard the words that the singer was singing—

> *In the Big Rock Candy Mountains*
> *There's a land that's fair and bright*
> *Where the handouts grow on bushes*
> *And you sleep out every night*

—he was screaming to be heard over the volcano of his own guitar, and behind him the drums were a war zone, but when I heard these words it was as if everything else fell away—

> *In the Big Rock Candy Mountains,*
> *The jails are made of tin*
> *And you can walk right out again,*
> *As soon as they put you in*

—and the singer and I were the only beings in existence, and there was nothing in creation but his voice singing and

my ears hearing him, and the fact of our relating in this way
was *the* fact of existence—

There ain't no short-handled shovels,
No axes, saws nor picks,
I'm bound to stay
Where you sleep all day,

—and every word he sang felt true to me, but there was
something devastating about this vision, where cops and jails
and bosses and dogs—that awful and immortal *they*—still figured so powerfully, foregrounded even in utopia, in Heaven—

Where they hung the jerk
That invented work
In the Big Rock Candy Mountains

—and I realized with shuddering clarity that the song
stirred my spirit in the same way that Holy things did, only
the song was a liar because it lied about Heaven and therefore
it was a disruption of Grace, the Devil's work, a limit, and
the hands that held me set me loose as the song finished—

I'll see you all this coming fall
in the Big Rock Candy Mountains

—and I landed uneasily on my feet, fell to my knees,
face hot—how many tears would I cry tonight? How much

sorrow is required of one who would bear the weight of the fallen world?—and stood up screaming—I don't know what I said, exactly—and pushing and shoving my way toward the front of the room, I needed to get to the microphone, had to *tell them*—what? I would know when I said it; Parker would speak through me and anything I said would be the right thing, but I had to get there—but people weren't getting out of my way anymore and somebody hit me with a closed fist and I reacted without thinking and struck back at that person but I missed him and hit somebody else and the whole place erupted and I was being martyred and my message—I was still screaming—swallowed and then a bouncer stood over me—I was on the floor again, there was some blood in my eyes—and it was his hands alone that were lifting me up, then held my hands fast behind me, I was stumbling, being frog-marched, angry faces cursing and spitting at me and leaning in close so I could hear them (I saw Anchor, a face in the crowd) and they were calling me things and I screamed back at them but couldn't hear, never knew, what it was that I said—

Then I was wandering the streets, bloody, alone as I had been on the night I was first saved. I could feel the punches I'd taken settling down from their fresh pain into an abiding soreness, bruises I felt no need to look at right away. Let Katy fret over them later. She surely would. My head was not clear so much as empty now; I felt hollowed out, a vessel, cored. *Lord, Parker, fill me up with your righteousness,* I thought.

Then I thought that maybe the best thing would be to try and for a while think nothing at all.

Thirteenth Street, then Eleventh, Ninth, Eighth, First, Main. Side streets. Alleys. Everything is a way station. Turnarounds. Cul-de-sacs. Access roads. Churches. Dark storefronts, the post office, the offices of the *Independent Florida Alligator* newspaper, a record store, the Masonic Temple, a couple of banks. Frat bars lit up in screaming neon or a lone light in the back of Emiliano's Italian restaurant by which the busboy mopped between tables now set only with their own flipped-over chairs. At the edge of the famous duck pond, where no fowl stirred on the face of the black water, and the bright bauble-moon was as clear below as above. Back on University Avenue—the lesbian bookstore, the drive-thru Taco Bell—where free shuttle buses provided by the school lurched up and down the street, to and from downtown, standing-room only and the aisles packed too with kids who sang fight songs and copped feels and filled that rolling drunk tank with their stinking puke. Construction sites. Angular skeletons of apartment buildings and planned communities, wired for broadband and satellite. *The Life You Save, indeed,* I thought, as I walked past it, headed vaguely back toward campus and my neighborhood but not yet ready to go home. Across the street from the plasma center's strip mall was a rent-to-own furniture store. I walked over to it, drawn like a bug to a porch light, though the store and its sign were both dark. I felt like I was really seeing it for what it was, this wellspring of human misery, the working poor

shackled to monthly payments, usurious rates, it was a suit-
able analog to the plasma center, and the intersection wanted
only for a check-cashing store to complete the unholy trinity.
I sat down on the sidewalk with my back against the white
stone façade of Planned Furnishings, across the street from
an empty lot marked only by a billboard that read CONSOLI-
DATED PROPERTIES. What could be said of a God that allowed
such horror in the world?

I wept.

The path of faith is a gravel road that spirals up a mountain
whose peak is lost to view. The sky is always gray on this
mountain, leaden and vast, marked only by the fog that ob-
scures the peak, but subtly infused with the bright light of
God's loving presence, which awaits those who make it to
journey's end. The path passes through a country so austere
it appears almost blighted, but this is because everything un-
necessary has been cast away—all the horrors of the world
as well as the dulcet delights of our utopia, that secret and
special place that God blesses but does not deign to visit.
The first stage of the journey had been to realize that there
was a world worth living in. The second stage had been to
actually come to life. The third and final stage was to give
all that up, of one's own righteous volition, for the only thing
that could possibly be better, which is to say, the only thing
in the universe that really existed at all.

From a certain windswept plateau, a resting place on the
path, I beheld the totality of Parker's vision: its scope and

magnificence matched that of this very mountain on which I stood, and yet, unlike with the mountain, I could see the fullness of what Parker had done. Through study and dedication I had reached his limit, and if I continued in my pursuit—as he was willing me to do, and as I, with all the purity of my longing heart, willed to do for him—then I would surpass him. Could this have been his intention all along? Was it the force of his desire that had brought me here?

In the distance above the summit of the mountain disappeared into more of the same gray, as if the sky were the skin of some great slain animal, hung up to dry. But I knew there was the golden-crimson firelight of eternal truth burning at the top for me, and that a shaft of flame fallen from that original pyre was what burned inside my own heart, and that this would draw me to the apex, the terminus of the lonely and faithful path. Likeness called out to rejoin with larger likeness, as all water flows to the ocean and—*say it again, say it again*—purity of heart is to will one thing, even as I walked down sidewalks lit sickly by streetlamps, a river of shadow dotted with islands of anemic orange light, in and out of traffic, horns and curses, the well-traveled route home overmapped with the lonely faith path, two places at once, Here and not-Here, as the Pattern is the breaking of the Pattern, left turn right turn the path is always straight and narrow, through the fence gate and up to the porch—the last door hinge since broken and the screen door junked in a tall green bush like a knife sticking out of a head—but I did not pass through the portal—I paused before the doorway, frozen, one foot extended, pressing for-

ward on open, empty air as if on a face of stone, exerting pressure on nothing, and this nothing unyielding, it rebuffed me,
and so finally I put my foot back down on the ground and
just stood there, unable to cross the threshold and step onto
the porch. I put a hand forward, palm out, but it would not
go through, either. I could feel a heightening of my senses, a
quickening in my blood.

The living room was dark, and the VW, too. I could have
called out, roused them up, but I stayed silent, and my silence
was the secret of the secret, the silence of the mystic rose that
was fully blossomed within me, the silence of the paradox at
the heart of faith.

I walked around the side of the house—the far side—
where Paolo's tent had been. When had he left us? How long
had he stayed? What time was it now? I tried the back door.
The knob was cool in my hand. I held a big breath, turned
it, and swung the door wide open. I stood in the warm sweep
of air as if in a tide pool, keeping still as it washed over me.
Then I stepped forward and once again the house wouldn't
have me. I could go no farther than the concrete slab on
which I stood.

Fishgut.

I turned away from the house, and at the moment I beheld the tent felt a wild and elating warmth rising up from
my chest. Looking down I saw that a prophecy, one of my
own, finally, had come to pass. The mark of my faith was
radiant, and had set my thin tee shirt aflame. I reached into
the embered ring and unmindful of the heat-bite pulled hard

with both hands and the garment, rent, fell away from my body; glowing cinders of fabric free-fell onto the carpet of dead leaves, so that soon the whole yard was lit up like a movie set, but my faith shined brighter still; I was a lighthouse, and lit my own way down the final steps of the Path; it led to my tent of course, where a candle was lit for me, its weak light pitiful compared to the light I was bearing, and when I reached it—only a few more steps now—I would snuff it out or else it would be absorbed into me—was there a difference?—and then I would zip the flap open and expel all the dead husks of the candles stored within, and leave behind a heap of broken glass humped like dirt on a refilled grave.

Parker would return when I returned, and I was coming. I was almost Here.

ANCHOR

When she first sees David he's aloft, above the crowd, arms and legs akimbo, face twisted into a vaguely painful-looking but mostly ecstatic mask. He floats closer and she thinks first how good it is to see him, then how glad she is, specifically, to see him here. She's always liked David. He's cool, and super dedicated to his scene, and it's kinda funny that he's come out tonight, actually, because she's been thinking about him. Ever since—what was it, Tuesday? Wednesday? Anyway. Since she wrote this poem that she thinks he'll like. A copy of it's folded up in her pocket. She had been planning to swing by the house after the show, have a beer with whoever was around, and either give David the poem or leave it for him—though of course she fully expected him to be there, since he basically never goes out. Which is why it's so cool that he's here. The poem isn't supposed to be anything special, or maybe it's a little special, okay. Just a *Hey man, been thinkin' of you.* But now here he is at Clasen's, kicking ass in the Dust Biters pit, which is no mean feat—for a pair of folkies, these guys fucking *bring it*—so maybe there's something after all to that weird book she helped the Fishgut kids do the layout on. What was that saying they had? Desire brings your something something to the truth . . . Fuck, she can't remember how it goes. She can hear the rhythm of it in her head, the familiar intonations of the absent words like silhouettes on a screen. Oh well. She'll have to flip through a copy when she's over there. Of course she could also always check the master file on her hard drive when she gets home.

As the song ends, David drops—is dropped—back into the crowd. The greatest things in life really are free, aren't they? She's nudging her way through the audience to go throw her arms around him, but then there's shouting up ahead, a scuffle breaks out, and now there's chaos: some people are surging forward, looking to get in on whatever it is, while others are scrambling backward, wanting no part. Anchor is caught between two groups headed in opposite directions, nearly loses her feet in the crash and sweep. By the time she realizes that it's David at the center of it all, the situation has reached its climax; they're throwing him out. She strains, short girl amid the gawking throb, to see him, and thinks he catches her gaze but can't be sure. What did he *do* exactly? It must be a misunderstanding. He'd been shouting something, but she couldn't make out what. Anyway, the whole thing's over and done now. He's been booted. Removed. Ejected. Tossed. Good-bye.

She's about to go after him, but the singer is starting to say something and she pauses to listen.

"Goddamn, Gene," the singer says, theoretically to the drummer though he's talking into the mic and looking out at the audience. "Some weird shit goes down every time we play this fucking town."

"Ain't that why we keep coming back?" the drummer says.

"Yer fuckin' A," says the singer. "Gaines. Ville. Yer fuckin' A."

The crowd goes nuts—just totally apeshit—and the band launches into their take on "Joe Hill's Casey Jones," which sets the whole room churning. Fists piston the air, a hundred drunk, sweaty kids shouting themselves hoarse, each believing in their heart that these guys will be so fucking famous soon, and how cool it will be to be able to tell people about having seen them, back when. And Anchor knows these things as well as anyone, but she also knows that if she were in David's position he'd be going after her right now, so she turns her back on the best punk rock band in the whole Southeast, walks out of the cramped, hot room, wipes sweat from her face with the back of one hand. She looks out the big front windows of the main room for any sign of David in the street. Not seeing him—it makes sense that he wouldn't stand right in front of the place—she gets a stamp from the bouncer and steps out into the crisp night, looks up and down the road for him walking. Nobody. Nothing. He's gone. What can she do? Back to the original plan, then; she'll see him later—after the show ends, and it's probably almost done. She should go back in and catch the rest of the set. Okay.

Two kickass encores, then the show's really over. Anchor's, you know, standing around smoking cigarettes or whatever, when the drummer walks up to her. *To her!* "Hi," he says. "I'm Gene."

"I know," she says, deadpan—God, she can be a doofus!—and he stares at her, but only for like a second, because then she gets it, says: "I'm Anchor."

"Where'd you get that name?"

"It's something my mom used to call me when I was a kid. It just, I don't know. Stuck."

"I think it's cool."

"Thanks. Great show."

"Thanks. You coming to the party?"

"What party? Now?"

"Yeah, we have some friends who have this house. On Eighth and Fifth. They call it the Palace of Zinn. Do you know the place?"

"I've—heard of it."

"Well, you should come. I think some other bands are gonna play."

"Okay."

"You want to ride with us?"

"Sure."

So you really can't blame her for not swinging by Fish-gut. There are like a million people there who can take care of David, and she'll go by tomorrow or something. Everyone knows you don't pass up a chance to party with the band.

There was this thing that Thomas used to say all the time—quoting someone, she's pretty sure: *You can't be neutral on a moving train.* And how easy would it have been to board that train and go with him? How wonderful and wild and great to just take off? Freedom and danger, a life together, itinerant farm work in the plains states; rail yards and freezing rain.

But when Thomas told her about his plans for them, Seattle, she had known instantly that she wasn't going with him, that it wasn't for her. And she'd known, furthermore, that this scheme was his way of offering the love she'd been trying to draw out in him all along, but now that it was hers for the taking she wasn't sure what to do with it, or if she even wanted it at all. And what did he want from her, anyway? She wasn't even twenty! She needed time, she said, to figure things out. There'd be other protests, plenty: the national party conventions, the G7, who knew what else. The movement was just getting going; it was going to be around a long time. And also, she was embarrassed to admit it, but what the hell: she *liked* school.

Poor Thomas! So reticent with his emotions (between explosions, that is), so guarded and exposed at once, so brusque yet so easy to wound. He was inconsolable, and to be honest a little bit scary, stomping his feet, shouting how he was going with or without her; but when she told him that she understood his decision and supported him, he bawled. *He doesn't want my admiration,* she remembers thinking. Which was a real shame, because it was all she'd had left to give him, except for farewell sex, which he first turned up his nose at, but in the end wasn't too proud to accept, and then they were both crying, and then first light punched through the tree cover, and he slung his backpack over his shoulder and walked away in the direction of the highway, leaving her behind, alone in his bed, where she rolled over and drowsed again—the last time she would ever sleep at Fishgut. Summer love!

She had worshipped them—all of them—sort of; what they seemed to stand for, who they seemed to be. She hadn't wanted to *be* them, exactly, but had hungered to feel things as powerfully as they did. And then that day came when she shared a dream with Katy, and they found the book and everything, and she actually felt like she had achieved the level they were at, however briefly. And it wasn't that she hadn't liked what she found there, or that she retreated out of fear. It was more like—how to phrase this?—even as she had given herself over fully to the experience, there was this other part of her that understood on some deeper level that the experience *of* the experience was a kind of capstone, not the dawn of a new era, as it clearly was for them. It was for her something fleeting and unknowable glimpsed on the horizon, a trick of the sunset light.

Helping out with the zine had been her going-away present to them, for everything they'd done for her, and because, truly, she wished them only the best. (Also, a good way to work on her design skills. The zine is in her portfolio now.) She *loved* them: Katy, David, Liz, and the whole messy rest, all the randoms and unknowns, the passers-through and the passing-through itself. She loved the way they talked, especially—how they gave full credence to ultimate concerns, the rhetoric a little windy, sure, but the passion undeniable, the attraction intense. They lived as if the fate of the very universe were perpetually at stake and in their hands.

Earnest Thomas on the one hand with his politics, the holy power trio and their minions on the other. It didn't take an Introduction to Dialectics (though she happens to be enrolled this semester in a class where they're giving her one) to see their antithetical positions as halves of a larger singularity: the desire for an encompassing horizon, a totalizing vision, an epistemology sufficient to enclose the whole known world, and account for everything unknown, too. A beautiful dream, impeccable and doomed, but honest—except in that it could never know itself as the parable, the myth it truly was.

But that was all so long ago. A lifetime, twelve months— eons! Think how much has happened since then. The Seattle protests, for example, were a huge success, with rioting and everything. Thomas was arrested on the very first day. He was masked up and helping direct some people who were trying to drive a dumpster through a Starbucks window. They held him for ten days and refused him treatment of a bruised rib and a badly sprained ankle, both courtesy, he said, of an aggressive paramilitary police force in full storm trooper regalia. The charges were dropped for whatever reason—he was small potatoes, or the fact that they had no evidence against him. He was too banged up to try freight-hopping, but managed somehow to stow away on Amtrak, where he befriended a retired couple in the dining car. They bought him all his meals for three straight days while he regaled them with stories, then, when the train rolled into Atlanta, gave him money to buy a Greyhound ticket to "go honest" for the rest of the way home. He thanked them, even hugged them, but pocketed the cash and snuck onto the Greyhound, too, because not taking full advantage of the obliviousness of disgruntled wage slaves was truly an insult to their alienation from their labor. He finally got back to Gainesville on the twentieth of December and hobbled home from the bus station. When he got there he found a burned-out hulk with its fence wreathed in yellow police tape, a Consolidated Properties sign out front, because not even a world-class SOB like Stuckins was going to rebuild from the ground up.

From the back room at Clasen's, he called all the people with her last name in the St. Johns County phone book and eventually reached her father, who sounded none too pleased to provide him with his ex-wife's phone number—but he did, and Thomas finally got hold of her, and she told him what she knew about what happened. It was five days till Christmas. What could she do? She invited him to her mother's, which was a whole fiasco in itself, the upshot of which was that she cut her visit short and the two of them spent NYE2K blowing the kindly train couple's money (and some of Anchor's father's) on a twenty-five-dollar-a-night road motel in Waldo, for all intents and purposes off the map, if not the grid.

After the world didn't end, Anchor said it was stupid of her to have left it like that with her mother, and she wanted to go back to Ponte Vedra and patch things up. Thomas, who wasn't exactly not invited, but whose presence certainly wouldn't make things easier, said he thought he'd go back to Gainesville and check on Liz, who was living with her mother again. Not long after school was back in session, he started crashing with Anchor at her dorm, which was okay until her roommate's boyfriend dumped her, because then Sheila started to pick up on how Thomas hung around even when Anchor was at class. Not wanting to seem uncool, Sheila held her peace for as long as she could stand to, and by the time she finally confronted her roommate, Anchor was actually relieved, even grateful, because her reunion with Thomas was way past its sell-by date, and the only thing keeping them together was inertia plus the fact that he had nowhere to go. Now he would have to figure something out, a new plan. Fuck it, he said, he was the king of new plans. She encouraged him to go see his family, and/or David's. He said he'd see where the wind blew him—some dumb shit like that.

But then he never went anywhere. He got his old job at Clasen's back, and a room opened up at the Palace of Zinn. They run into each other sometimes, and either say hello or don't.

In August she cut her dreadlocks off and dyed her buzz cut red.

Around that same time she started volunteering two afternoons a week at Bread and Roses, a local not-for-profit women's health center. She helps out with paperwork and takes phone calls. Anti-choice fanatics crowd the sidewalk out front, holding up posters of mangled fetuses and shrieking like campus evangelists, which, she assumes, some of them also are. The women come in stone-faced and spooked, lower lips quivering, or else cursing blue streaks. Anchor talks to them, sometimes about what they're going through but usually not; usually it's just, "Hey, how are you" and whatever. Mundane chatter calms them down.

It feels good to be part of something. To know you are doing right, not for the whole world, maybe, not all at once, but for this woman, for that one, for yourself. It was hard at first to balance the volunteering with her classes, but she's gotten the hang of things, made it over the hump of midterms, and is pretty much cruising along.

It is November, another November. Today is election day.

It's dark in her dorm room, but bright outside. A sun-line limns the borders of the heavy shade. Anchor's first class is at 11:05, which is in an hour and a half. After class she's going straight to the clinic, so if she's going to vote, she should really go do it first thing. There's a polling place right in Turlington Hall.

Despite all their personal drama, Thomas is still basically her model of an Authentic Anarchist, and he would say—indeed, has said—that voting is more than merely a waste of time, it's *irresponsible*, which is the worst thing an anarchist can be. By engaging with the system on its terms, by believing the lie, you help legitimize and perpetuate something fundamentally illegitimate. He says. And, who knows, on some level it might even be true. On the other hand—and this, for her, is the kicker—it's the first election she's ever been eligible to vote in, and it's one of those things you grow up imagining yourself doing, and now she wants to do it. That might not be the greatest, most ethically sound reason, but it's hers.

She wants to see if the booth will actually look like she imagines.

It doesn't.

She always thought of it as a quiet space, sealed off, maybe like an old-timey phone booth, but this thing is a gray plastic table—like from a Fisher-Price set—standing on spindly metal legs in the bustling ground-floor lobby of Turlington Hall. The privacy curtain is blue and looks like it should be dividing first class from coach. It doesn't even hang as low as her waist. But she's in there, pen in hand, looking over the list of mostly strange names. All politics is local—they're always saying that at the clinic—but here she is not knowing who most of these people are or what they stand for. As a kid she never thought about all the minor stuff, ballot measures and constitutional amendments and whatnot. What does a comptroller even *do*? She always imagined the ballot as a single question written in direct address. ANCHOR, WHO DO YOU

WANT THE PRESIDENT TO BE? So okay, forget the whole rest of it. This one at least is a no-brainer; she may be wrong to be here at all but she can at least mitigate the damage by voting her conscience. And anyway she isn't sure that Thomas is right about this. Refusal too is action; there is no way to be in the world without being part of it.

She remembers how David and Katy didn't want a website. What would they say if they could know that there are five sites now? Anchor doesn't involve herself, doesn't post on their boards or check regularly for updates, but she knows what's out there, more or less. Splinter sects have emerged, with conflicting creeds and tenets, mostly centering on the one question Parker seems never to have considered: that of who the "real" prophet is, or was, and how to choose one over the rest, or else the whole holy rabble en masse. Some see Parker as Christ's agent, therefore underling; others say Parker was (or is, since he's still MIA) Christ's successor, therefore supplanter; and others still identify David as the true and chosen exponent of the gospel of anarchy, all the more pure for having left behind no book and no body, nothing but rumors and ash.

A thought passes through her mind—*Desire is a strange attractor. Your longing warps the arc of the world's emergent truth*—as she darkens the bubble for Nader, slips the ballot into the slot, exits the booth, and walks off to have her day. She does all the things that she planned to do, then heads from Bread and Roses to Leonardo's, the hipster pizza place that they always used to dumpster from. She's meeting this guy there. After dinner, they decide to take a little walk, and end up at this record store where she picks up the new Radiohead album, which she heard playing at a coffee shop a few days ago, and even though she doesn't usually go in for electronica, there's something . . . different about this. She can't say what exactly, but there'll be plenty of time to figure it out, because she owns it now. It's in her purse. Since they're basically next door to the Shamrock already, they decide to have a couple of drinks, and then it's getting kind of late, so.

"You feel like walking me home?" she asks him.

"Yeah, that sounds good."

And why shouldn't it? Good is this guy's whole thing. He's funny, attentive, sweet to her, etc. So what if he pledged a frat freshman year? He's not in it anymore. They share a kiss good night—not just a quick peck, either; a *good* one—but she doesn't invite him up. She has before, and she will again, but not tonight. Tonight she sleeps alone, and happens to dream a particular dream, the only recurring dream she's ever had. It has come with irregular and (mercifully) diminishing frequency over the past year. She expects it will come less and less often the more time goes by, but she knows in her heart that it will never entirely go away.

In the dream, like in real life, she slips out of the party with Gene around two-thirty. They're both hammered and nearly tumble as they attempt to navigate the Palace of Zinn's three paint-stripped front steps, because they're not looking where they're going, because they're kissing like kissing is the only thing left in the world as they make their stumbling way to the '88 Chevy Astro van that is the Dust Biters' tour bus.

Gene slides the side door open and hands her into the vehicle with adorable cartoonish chivalry. But in the dream it's different: she doesn't enter the van, lets go of his hand, tells him that she's very sorry but there's something she has to go do.

He slides the door shut behind them, together alone finally, all clothing hustled into the discard pile, every breath and murmur swelling to fill the close, closed space. But in the dream, what happens instead is there's a close-up of Gene, startled, concerned for her or maybe just blue-balled—who can tell with these band guys?—then cut to a long aerial shot of her running down Fifth Avenue toward Thirteenth Street.

Hungover in the dawn light in the van, she finds Gene, still naked, fiddling with a yellow disposable camera that he might have done who knows what with while she was sleeping, prone, exposed.

"Give me the camera."

"Oh c'mon, I just—"

"Give it to me or I'll start screaming."

"Okay, fuck, Jesus, I thought you were cool."

Instead of that, this: she's a dark streak cutting through the Gainesville night, covering football field lengths in eye-blink time, but the streets aren't linking up where they're supposed to, so it's a complete surprise when she turns an unfamiliar corner and Fishgut, burning, erupts into view. She stands there, a lone figure at the far end of a deserted street, staring at a house on fire. All she can do is bear witness for what always feels like forever. In dreams the thread of time is unstrung from its loom; there's no way to gauge or measure the interval. Eventually, inevitably, she will be released into consciousness, jolt awake shaking, chest quaking, sweaty all over, jaw clenched. But that's later. No matter how long the dream lasts, the house is never consumed. And this is the point of the dream, maybe, what she believes or would like to be able to: that as long as she is there to watch it, the burning house can't burn down.

On mornings after Anchor has the dream, she always does the same thing. She makes herself get out of bed and then she opens the shade, so the light dazzles her sleep-crusted eyes and floods the whole room with sun. Then she gets down on her knees in front of her twin bed, closes her eyes, clasps her hands before her, and bows her head. Lucky that Shelia's not around. She doesn't pray for, or to, anything in particular—doesn't use words at all, in fact, not even in her mind—only holds the posture for as long as she wants to, whatever feels right. When she's ready she stands back up and goes over to her desk. She sits down at the desk and opens the bottom drawer on the right side, where, in a repurposed sandwich bag with a color-seal slider (blue and yellow make green) is the folded-up paper that was in her pocket the night of the Dust Biters show. She unzips the bag and pulls the paper out, unfolds it, and reads the words. They're her own. It's the poem she never showed David, and it goes like this:

Song

Fertilize the worst and lose the ground.
Better to become opposition together—
Standing apart and in the way. We
Are named Origin Myth. Anything
Beautiful and furious which refuses
Is our Song
      Sung in love and grass and sun.
To live even in time without limit.
No blood for the true faith.
An old monument falls down forever.
We are the young world screaming *Grace*.

AUTHOR'S NOTE

This novel is set in the real city of Gainesville, Florida, where I lived from 2000 to 2004. While some of the locations, businesses, landmarks, etc., really exist or existed (though, of course, they are used fictitiously), others are entirely made up, and still others exist in a kind of composite reality, as in the case of the planet statues that Katy rides past on her bicycle. These statues, which together comprise the Gainesville Solar Walk, are the work of a regional artist named Elizabeth Indianos. They were erected in 2002, but I was determined to have them in my Gainesville, even though that meant dislocating them slightly in time. Similarly, the nondenominational Baughman Meditation Center on Lake Alice would have been under construction during the main action of this novel; it was opened to the public in 2000. Clasen's, unfortunately, does not exist, though hope springs eternal.

The excerpts from Parker's journal are also composites synthesized (and/or collaged) from a wide variety of sources, some publicly available, others not. Parker's politics, in particular, owe a great deal to the works of the CrimethInc. Collective. In addition to the passage that appears as this book's first epigraph, paraphrases, bastardizations, intentional perversions of, and unattributed direct quotes from their various books, pamphlets, and communiqués abound throughout Parker's writings. Since all CrimethInc. works are anticopyright and published anonymously, I felt free and even encouraged to plagiarize and pirate as I saw fit. Also, though CrimethInc. has been around since the mid-1990s, their major works have all been published in the twenty-first century, beginning with *Days of War, Nights of Love* in 2001. A True Believer might speculate, therefore, that the Good Zine (or Parker himself, still unaccounted for) had some formative influence on their thinking, rather than the other way round.

One last thing. Parker's image of the diamond necklace that becomes the diamond garrote is from Paul Violi's poem "I.D., or Stolen Identities." Ironically, it is the only thing in this book borrowed *with* permission, and I thank Paul for granting me the use of his words.

ACKNOWLEDGMENTS

To the following people I offer my deepest gratitude for friendship, attention, love, employment, patience, and general heroism: Danielle Benveniste, Blake Butler, Joshua Cohen, Elliott David, Rachel Fershleiser, Bill Hayward, Andrew Leland, Peter Masiak, Amy McDaniel, Amy Mees, Gene Morgan, Amanda Peters, Robert Polito, Jeremy Schmall, Michael Signorelli, Eva Talmadge, Maggie Tuttle, Mark Wagner; my parents and my sister, Melanie; and the Taylor and Starkman families.

A special thanks to Caryn and Andrew Goldner, who make sure that I get out of Brooklyn from time to time, and in whose home portions of this book were written.

BOOKS BY JUSTIN TAYLOR

Everything Here Is the Best Thing Ever

Stories

ISBN 978-0-06-188181-7 (PAPERBACK)

"Justin Taylor is a master of the modern snapshot."
—Los Angeles Times

"Superb . . . Each story is spare and clean and speaks the truth in beautiful resonant prose"
—Publishers Weekly

The Word Made Flesh

Literary Tattoos from Bookworms Worldwide

Edited by Eva Talmadge and Justin Taylor

ISBN: 978-0-06-199740-2 (PAPERBACK)

A full-color, beautifully packaged guide to the emerging subculture of literary tattoos, based upon photographs of the best and weirdest literary tattoos submitted to the authors, including quotations from favorite writers, beloved lines of verse, literary portraits, and illustrations.